INTO THE REALM

(THE CALL OF THE ROSE-BOOK ONE)

BY

CHANELLE NASH

This book is dedicated to my Grandmothers.

Whom had passed away before this books conception,
but I think they both would have enjoyed the read.

Love and Miss you both heaps.

Chapter One

Jordan stood by the back door of his mother's kitchen. One hand in his jeans pocket and the other nursing a pint of larger for the past hour. He had only taken a mouthful from it because half of him just wanted to go home and at the same time, home was the last place he wanted to go.

Looking over the crowded kitchen in search of his mother and sisters all he could see was a sea of female faces. They were glancing at him every few minutes. Their ages varying from fourteen up. They were all friends of his three sisters and mother. The younger ones would go bright red and into a fit of giggles if he so much as glanced at them, never mind smiled. The older ones always clearly made their intentions known.

He normally loved the attention and would partake in a bit of harmless flirting with the older ones, but tonight he just wasn't in the mood. If it wasn't his sisters eighteenth birthday, he wouldn't be here now. Even some of his mother's friends kept giving him the eye. He politely smiled at them while internally shuddering at the thought.

"Penny for your thoughts," a female voice asked at his side, a voice he knew all too well.

Jordan looked down his side noticing his mother was smiling up at him. He was a foot taller than his mother was but she was definitely a force to be reckoned with. "They're not worth a penny," he replied giving her a small smile.

"Jordan sweetie," his mother said looking him over. "Why are you still in your leather jacket? Aren't you hot in that?"

"Just a tad, but I'm kind of under orders not to remove it," Jordan said noticing his sisters were heading towards them.

"And whose orders were those?" his mother asked.

"Ours," three voices chimed at once. Jordan's mother spun around on her heels so fast she would have fallen, had Jordan not grabbed her arm to steady her.

Isabella looked at her daughters standing in front of her. She looked back at Jordan who was looking at the ceiling pretending to whistle. Gathering herself, she turned her attention back to her daughters.

"Why on earth is your brother not allowed to take off his coat?" she asked looking slightly confused.

"Do you want females fainting all over the place?" Jessica said, as a smirk spread across her face.

"What the hell are you talking about?" Isabella said giving her oldest daughter a stern look which included her two other daughters.

"Mum, we are cursed to have a gorgeous brother, with a nice bod. His very presence makes the girls swoon."

"Have you been reading romances again?" Isabella asked while trying not to snicker.

"Yes, but that's not the point," Jessica replied. "If Jordan takes his jacket off, we will have Joanne's friends going into giggles. Janice's friends will be swooning and trying to flirt with him and my friends, well we already know half of them want to jump his bones."

"Don't be ridiculous," snapped Isabella at her daughter.

"And let's not forget about some of your friend's mum." Jessica couldn't help adding that bit, knowing it would wind her mother up. Isabella looked at her son, ignoring Jessica and the nods of agreement she got from Janice and Joanne. She hated it when her daughters teamed up.

"Jordan, you do remember you are the oldest, don't you"?

"Yes," Jordan replied giving his mother a confused look.

"And you haven't told them to get stuffed, like you would normally do?" Isabella looked at her daughters smirking faces and then turned her attention back to Jordan.

"Hang on a minute, *who* told you to not remove your jacket?"

"Nobody *told* me, as you put it," Jordan replied.

"So who was it that *asked* you not to remove your coat? Or is that a stupid question?" Isabella had the feeling she already knew the answer.

"Charlotte did," Jordan said flatly. His face was void of emotions. Isabella still noticed the slight gleam in his eye whenever Jessica's best friend was mentioned, even if he didn't realise he was doing it.

Isabella let out a frustrated breath and turned towards her daughter's, she pointed her finger at each of them sternly. "You three have got to stop doing that."

"Doing what?" the girls said at the same time faking looks of surprise, like they didn't know what their mother was talking about.

"You know bloody well what I'm talking about," Isabella said glaring at the three of them. "Now, Joanne you go and keep your teeny bopper friends away from your brother. As sweet as it is that he is their first crush, he is too old for them. I'm pretty sure the last thing he needs or wants right now is a bunch of fourteen to sixteen-year-old girls giggling all over him."

"Yes mum," Joanne said in a little girl voice, the one she used when she was being punished.

"Oh and Joanne," Isabella said raising an eyebrow at her youngest daughter.

"Yes mum," Joanne answered stopping mid stride and turning around.

"No alcohol, you're only fifteen. If you or any of your friends are tempted so much as to sneak a sip, I will confine you all to your bedroom until their parents get here to pick them up. Then you my dear Joanne will be grounded, do I make myself clear?" she said putting her hands on her hips. She had already stopped a couple of them sneaking out to the garden with some vodka cruisers.

"Yes mum," Joanne replied before turning on her heels and heading towards a group of girls dressed in jeans and baggy t-shirts.

Turning her attention back to her other daughters Isabella continued, "Janice darling, how much have you had to drink?" she asked noticing her daughter having trouble standing.

"I don't know, I haven't been counting," Janice replied grabbing onto Jessica's shoulder to keep herself steady.

"Go and enjoy your birthday," Isabella said. "However don't come complaining to me when you're hugging the toilet and your head is pounding," she said smiling. She watched Janice give her a funny look before heading straight for the fridge.

"She will learn the hard way," Isabella said aloud. She turned her attention back to her eldest daughter and with a stern look on her face she continued, "And you."

"What," Jessica said standing up as straight as she could in the six-inch-high heels she was wearing.

"Don't what me, you should know better." Isabella took a few steps closer to her daughter and with the loud music playing she was out of Jordan's hearing range. "How many times do I have to tell you and your sisters, not to use Charlotte on your brother to get your own way?"

"Loads, but it works so well. He always does as she asks him and with no questions asked."

"And I suppose Charlotte asked him to stay by the back door as well?" Isabella asked. She had noticed her son hadn't moved from the spot since he'd arrived.

"Not that I know of…why?"

"No reason," she said catching sight of Charlotte. The look on the young woman's face was telling. "You might want to go and get Charlotte away from that young man over there, the look on her face says she's about to thump him one."

"I'm on it," Jessica said as she headed towards her friend who was standing with her ex-boyfriend.

Isabella turned her attention back to her son with concern. She could see he was angry so she walked the short distance to where he stood.

"What is it?" she asked him standing on his left.

"What the hell is she doing here?" Jordan asked with anger in his voice. He looked so hurt starring out into the crowd. "And with him," he said motioning to the pair.

Isabella looked out over the people. A very attractive woman with ash blonde hair stood there. Her hair was curled to her shoulders and she was wearing a very revelling top. It was Sonya, her son's ex-girlfriend as of two weeks ago. This was not going to end well. She looked back at Jordan and noticed the clench of his jaw. It was clenched so tightly she thought he might break his teeth if he didn't stop soon. To make matters worse Sonya had turned up with Michael, her new lover and Jordan's best friend.

"I don't know, but in our defence the invites for tonight were sent out months ago. With all the various preparations for things, it must have slipped our minds too un-invite her. It was only two weeks ago that you split up," Isabella said. She didn't really know what else to say.

"Yeah we split up and she has still turned up," he replied through gritted teeth.

"Jordan you two were together for ten years, maybe she came here to celebrate Janice's eighteenth birthday like everyone else."

"So who invited Michael?"

"Nobody did, Janice doesn't really know him. In all honesty I think that she's only here to rub it in and get at you." She looked from Jordan to Sonya and back again. "Tell you what, go find one of Jessica's friends and do some harmless flirting."

"What!!" Jordan said looking at his mother in surprise.

"You heard me. Sonya would only have brought Michael to rub it in your face. If you notice, she isn't all over him at the moment. Wait until she actually notices you, then her actions will change. So a bit of harmless flirting won't kill you. It's not like I'm telling you to take them upstairs and screw their brains out."

"And whom should I be flirting with, mother." Jordan whispered in her ear as he moved to the other side of her, closer to the table. His tone was too calm for her liking.

"I don't know Lisa, Samantha, Miranda, pick one," she said looking at him sternly. "Just not Charlotte."

Jordan raised his eyebrows in surprise. "Ok…so why not Charlotte?"

"Well let's forget for a second that you, I and everyone else knows that Charlotte has always had a thing for you. She has also known you long enough to know if you did start flirting with her, something was going on. Do you really want to use her affections like that, just to get back at Sonya?" Isabella asked, already knowing what her son was going to say.

"No. Of course not."

"Well then, plus if you smiled at Charlotte it would piss Sonya off any way. By the way, you not telling anyone that you split up with her hasn't really helped the situation," she said giving her son a stern look.

"Doesn't matter any way," replied Jordan as his eyes wandered from his mother.

"Why?" she asked.

"Charlotte is on her way over here," he replied, his lips curling into a small smile.

Isabella looked over at the young woman carrying two mugs of what she would assume was coffee. A big smile was plastered all over her face. Charlotte always had a big smile for everyone, no matter who it was. The ones she directed at Jordan were different though. They always made her face glow, like she was being lit from within.

Isabella couldn't help notice Sonya sliding her hand around Michael's arm and placing her head on his shoulder. She had clearly noticed where Jordan was standing. They looked like an odd couple and Isabella couldn't help the snicker that escaped when she saw Sonya's angry face. Isabella guessed Sonya must have just spotted Charlotte heading towards Jordan so she was also heading their way. The closer she got the more lovey-dovey she got with Michael. Isabella wasn't buying it, anger laced Sonya's face and she could see it even though there was a fake smile plastered there. She hated it when she was right. Without giving it a second thought, she decided to leave Jordan to it. She had to make sure her under age daughter was behaving her little self.

Chapter Two

Jordan vaguely noticed his mother's hasty exit from the kitchen, out of the corner of his eye. He watched as Charlotte headed towards him. He could swear she was in a different outfit earlier. She was currently wearing fitted tight black jeans with a white shiny belt with rhinestones on it. They were sparkling as the light hit it. The black sequined top she wore was also sparkling under the lights. The top was slightly low cut and showed she had cleavage, but wasn't too revealing. Her blonde curls hung lightly over her padded shoulders in her usual half up, half down hair style. Her fringe was teased and no doubt had too much hair spray. He swore she was going for the Samantha Fox look. He couldn't help but smile to himself as he pictured Jessica and Charlotte dancing around the kitchen singing 'Touch Me' at the top of their lungs.

"This is for you," Charlotte said, stopping at his side and handing him one of the mugs.

"Thanks," Jordan replied smiling at her. He opened his mouth to say something but she cut him off.

"You haven't really touched your larger so I figured you weren't in a drinking mood. I grabbed you a coffee instead. White with two sugars," she said smiling.

"Aren't you drinking?" he asked taking notice of her coffee as well.

"Nah, I had a few Archers and lemonade earlier. I've had my drink to celebrate Janice's birthday."

"Fair enough then," Jordan said. He noticed her blood shot eyes. "Have you been crying?" he asked with concern.

"Just a little."

"Why?" he asked frowning.

"That bastard Tony turned up with his slut," Charlotte replied seething with hurt and anger.

"Isn't Tony your boyfriend?" Jordan said confused.

"We split up."

"I'm sorry to hear that, but why did you split up?"

"Because he is a two-timing git and he split up with me."

"Ok then," Jordan said surprised. That was the last thing he expected to hear. "Why would he do that, I thought you two got on great?"

"We did, until I refused to have sex with him. He cheated on me and I conveniently caught him in the act," she said trying to hide the hurt she felt. Jordan had known Charlotte for too long and could tell when she was hurting just by looking at her. Even when she tried to hide it, like she was doing now.

"Okay, so what is he even doing here? If you guys have split up?"

"One of Janice's friends got grounded and wasn't allowed to come unless chaperoned by her big brother. Ten points for guessing who the big brother happens to be," she finished with a snarky smile.

"Come here," he said as he pulled her into his arms. He took extra care not to spill his coffee on her. He knew how much she was hurting and had a deep need to comfort her.

"Well that didn't take long," snapped a venomous voice, interrupting them both.

Still holding Charlotte tightly to his chest, he turned his head towards the voice he knew so well. Sonya stood there with her arms folded over her chest and a smug look on her face. Anger was seething from her blue eyes. He had seen that look more times than he could count especially when he was near Charlotte. *What the hell was her problem?'* he thought. He looked from Sonya back to Charlotte. Charlotte's arms were nestled tightly around his waist and he knew straight away what Sonya was thinking.

Twisting his body, he grabbed Charlotte's mug from behind him. He placed both mugs on the glass top kitchen table next to him, never taking his eyes off Sonya for a minute. He still hadn't removed Charlotte's arms from around his waist.

"Sonya," Jordan said. His tone was flat and void of any emotion.

"Jordan and oh what was your name again," Sonya said. Her voice filled with venom as she gave a sly, sadistic smile to Charlotte.

"You know damn well what her name is," Jordan replied with anger in his tone. This seriously couldn't be the woman he had spent ten years of his life with. He couldn't believe the amount of anger, hatred and jealousy showing on Sonya's once beautiful face. Now she just looked decrepit and evil and all of it focussed on Charlotte.

He had been looking out for Charlotte since she was five years old. He protected her just as he did his sisters. He wasn't about to let his jealous ex-girlfriend harm or upset her, especially at his sister's birthday party. Putting his arm around Charlotte's shoulders protectively, he glared at Sonya not at all trusting what she would do.

"Oh that's right…Charlotte isn't it. The ever present thorn in my side during our relationship. Tell me Jordan how long did it take you to go running to her? Ten minutes or two hours?" Sonya asked while glaring at him.

"What is she talking about?" Charlotte whispered, clearly confused.

"Nothing for you to worry about," he replied, giving her a small smile.

"Don't pretend you don't know," Sonya snapped overhearing Charlotte's question.

"What do you want?" Jordan snapped. He felt Charlottes body tense next to him. He knew it was out of anger, not fear. She had removed her arm from around his waist and was examining her fingernails. He had known her long enough to know that was a sign she was getting ready for a fight. Unlike his sister Jessica who was fists and kicks, Charlotte was the classic stereotype. Nails, hair pulling, biting, the works. With the way Sonya was acting it wouldn't surprise him if she suddenly lunged for Charlotte. That's what would happen if Charlotte didn't go for her first. The last thing he wanted was to deal with was a cat fight right now.

"I see you avoided my question, so I will take that as ten minutes then," she said with fury lacing every word.

Taking a deep breath to contain the rage building within him, he looked intently at Sonya. "I will ask you again…what do you want?" he said, gritting his teeth. He couldn't help notice the smug smile that graced her lips. His one-time best friend stood behind her. She looked up at him and something flashed in her eyes. Instinctively he slowly pulled Charlotte behind him. He folded his arms across his chest and narrowed his eyes at Sonya, waiting for her to answer his question.

"I was invited," she replied defiantly.

"I believe the invitation was for you and me. Not me on my own and you with your new lover," Jordan replied.

"Michael's your best friend," Sonya said as she reached behind her to grab his hand. "So why wouldn't he be invited."

"Was my best friend and maybe he didn't get invited because it's Janice's birthday and she doesn't really know him. Hell you only got an invitation because you were with me at the time. She doesn't really know either of you, so why would she want you here on her special day? Come to think of it, I actually want nothing to do with him or you. I suggest you leave," Jordan replied, folding his arms.

"Or what…. you going to get Mummy and Daddy to remove me from the premises," Sonya said with a smirk. She thought she had the upper hand over Jordan.

"No, I won't have too," Jordan replied. He noticed Jessica out of the corner of his eye, watching the confrontation. He knew it wouldn't be long before she started heading over to them.

"And why is that," Sonya drawled sarcastically.

"Jessica is currently on her way over here and you know what she's like. Hit first then ask questions later." He tapped his finger on his chin as if he was thinking about something and continued. "I wonder what she will do when she gets over here and notices her brother acting protective over her best friend."

"You wouldn't let her touch me," said Sonya with worry. She had had many a run in with Jessica over the years.

Jordan laughed sardonically. "Is that fear I see flash before your eyes. Oh yes that's right, you can't take on Jessica and come out the victor. What do you think will happen when Jessica gets here and jumps you? Obviously Charlotte will join in and even though I have the strength to hold them both back, why would I want too?"

"It would spoil Janice's birthday if there was fight," Sonya replied smugly.

"True, however both Janice and Joanne would just join in. Even with Janice in her very intoxicated state," Jordan replied raising his eyebrows at her.

"Michael will defend me," Sonya said clearly grabbing at straws now.

"Like he has been since you came over here?" Jordan said. He shot a quick glance towards Michael before turning his attention back to Sonya. "He wouldn't dare touch a hair on any of my sister's heads."

"And why wouldn't he defend the woman he loves?" Sonya asked. Hoping those words would rile Jordan up.

"Because my love, Michael knows that I will floor him. He may love you as you put it, but let me tell you this. He is more than welcome to my sloppy seconds."

"How dare you," Sonya spat with anger.

"How dare I, seriously!! You are nothing more than a lying, cheating, deceitful, no-good slag, who always jumps to the wrong conclusions. Now get out of my parents' house before Jessica gives you a fat lip and Charlotte scratches your eyes out. All while I enjoy the show," Jordan said looking at her defiantly.

"This isn't over," she said with a murderous look, before turning around and heading towards the front door.

"Oh yes, it is sweetheart," Jordan yelled after her. He turned his body back slightly to make sure Charlotte was alright. He couldn't help but wince at the glare she was giving him.

"What the hell was that?" Charlotte asked slightly angry.

"What was what?" Jordan replied, giving her a smile.

"Don't you smile at me Jordan Jason Elfin," she said putting her hands on her hips. "Now tell me exactly why I suddenly went on alert and why I wanted to smack that tart. I haven't done anything to that bitch, so what's her bloody problem?"

Before Jordan could say anything Jessica came up beside Charlotte.

"Hey, what's going on?" she asked looking between the two of them.

"Jordan was about to enlighten me on what that prat Sonya's problem is?" Charlotte replied never taking her eyes from Jordan's.

Jordan couldn't believe it, now he had two sets of eyes glaring at him. They really are both as bad as each other sometimes. "What's there to tell, we split up and she automatically assumed that we were together," he said gesturing between himself and Charlotte.

"Just because you were giving me a hug, how pathetic can you get," Charlotte said frowning.

"In-it though," replied Jessica.

"You know what I mean," Charlotte replied. 'Hang on, you two have split up?"

"Yes," Jordan replied then continued quickly, noticing they were about to ask another question. "Two weeks ago, I caught her cheating on me with Michael. Does that answer the questions about to fly out of your gobs?"

"Oh Jordan," both girls said in unison as they wrapped their arms around him.

Placing his arms around their shoulders, he looked at each girl in turn. "Come on let's go enjoy the rest of the party shall we and see how shit faced Janice has gotten?"

Chapter Three

Jordan sat at the kitchen table the next morning, enjoying the full English breakfast before him. He looked around at his family and the three additions that were friends of each of his sisters. He couldn't help smirking at Janice who had her head on the table. She was moaning something about her head hurting. Her friend Sandra was also moaning about her head although all Jordan could see was her jet-black hair with streaks of red, purple, blue and yellow in it. He was surprised that Janice hadn't done anything like that to her hair yet.

He noticed that Joanne was giving him dirty looks while elbowing her red headed friend Sarah. She was blushing so much that you could hardly see the freckles on her face. Maybe he shouldn't have worn a singlet this morning, he thought to himself.

Sitting next to him was Jessica. Charlotte was the other side of her. They were having a whispered heated discussion. He couldn't hear what was being said between the girls but since they kept firing looks his way, he guessed it was about him. Probably due to the events of last night.

Sitting at the head of the table was Jordan's father. His dad was smirking at Janice in-between bites of his fried bread. Opposite him at the table was his mother sipping her mug of coffee, she looked to be in deep thought.

"Mum," Jordan said.

"Yes darling," his mother replied looking at him.

"Was great Uncle Theodore at the party last night?" Jordan asked.

"No, he had some stuff to do and couldn't make it." Isabella said looking at her son suspiciously. "Why?"

"No reason, I was just wondering?" Jordan replied shrugging.

"Jordan," Isabella said putting her mug down. "Spit it out." She knew there was a reason for his question, since Jordan never asked after her brother.

"Fine, I was just wondering if he'd moved into Rose Manor yet?"

"No he hasn't. Something come up so he can't move there yet, why?" Isabella asked. She had a hunch on why he wanted to know but thought she would ask anyway.

"I was thinking of heading up there for a while," he said nonchalantly. Jordan noticed the fear that crossed his mother's face. He also felt the hot liquid now coating his arm as his father spat out his drink. Wiping his arm on his singlet, he looked at his parents. "Is that a problem?"

"No sweetheart," Isabella replied trying to hide the fear building inside her. It wasn't time for Jordan to go to the house yet. It would be up to her to try to talk him out of it, but by the look on her son's face that may not be an easy task. He could be stubborn as hell when he wanted to be. "So when did this come about?" she tentatively asked.

"I have been thinking about it for the past two weeks. I hate staying at my flat and fancy a change of scenery."

"So why don't you stay here for a few weeks?" Isabella suggested smiling at her son.

"I really want to get out of London and be by myself for a while."

"Sweetheart I don't think you being on your own is the best thing right now. You are very emotional and I wouldn't want you to dwell on things."

"Mother."

"What?" Isabella replied.

"I won't be on my own to dwell on things. I will, in fact, be using the time to work. If I didn't know better, I would swear you were trying to talk me out of staying at the house."

"Why would I be trying to talk you out of going to Rose Manor?"

"I don't know, but that's what it seems like and you know how much I love it there."

"That was when you were little," she whispered.

"Little my arse, we stayed there two years ago."

"Fine you loved being at the house, but it won't be the same. You haven't stayed there since my parents passed on last year."

"Well, it's time I headed back to the house then aint it," Jordan said sitting back in his chair. He was getting a little annoyed at his mother's persistence.

"Well since there is no talking you out of it, when were you going to head up there?"

"I don't know? In a couple of day's maybe," he replied shrugging. "Actually if Uncle Theodore isn't going to move into the house then I might as well, save it being empty."

"You have gone from wanting to stay there for a few days, to moving there in the space of a couple of minutes," Isabella said looking at her son in shock.

"Sure why not. We all have a key to the place and Nan did say I could live there whenever I wanted. Now feels like the right time to do just that."

Isabella looked at her son, wondering if he was fully aware of the way that sounded. She knew that he would be feeling drawn to the house, but it was still too soon for him to go.

"Well can you at least give it a few weeks? I mean you have to organise movers for your stuff and sort out what you are going to do with your flat."

Jordan picked up his breakfast plates and walked around the table to stand next to his mother. "I'll think about it," he said as he placed a kiss on the top of her head.

Isabella watched her son put his plate in the sink and walk out of the room. She hadn't even noticed that the girls had left the room or when. She turned her attention back to her husband and fixed him with a glare.

"What?" Richard said in response.

"Well you could have said something."

"And what exactly should I have said," Richard asked, frowning at his wife.

"The truth as to why he can't go to the house yet."

"Oh yeah, because telling him the house has portals to other realms, one of which he is the prince of, would have gone down really well…. Not"

"Well you still have to tell him all that anyway."

"Yes and I will, but not yet. So what if he goes to the house early? I mean it's not like he is going to fall through one of the portals. I wouldn't worry about it. What is the worst that can happen?" Richard said as he got up and headed out of the room.

"FAMOUS LAST WORDS," Isabella yelled after him.

Chapter Four

Jordan slowly drove towards the large cottage that had been in his family for generations. It was the first time he'd been there since his grandparents passing last year. He usually wasn't on his own. Every summer his family would come up here and spend six weeks with a few friends, usually Charlotte. When Sonya came with them, she usually could only stay for a couple of weeks. She always had to get back to work.

Last year was also the first time he could remember his family hadn't spent the summer at the house. Jordan guessed it was because emotions were still raw from his grandparents passing which was only a few weeks before summer break. He would have to visit their graves and pay his respects while he was there. They were buried in a family plot on the grounds.

It was a pleasant drive up to the house. The trees that lined the path looked recently trimmed, which allowed the spring sun to shine through.

Bringing his silver Mercedes to a stop on the gravel drive outside the house he pulled out his mobile and pressed one on speed dial. "Hey mum, just thought I would let you know…."

"You're at the house aren't you?" his mother interrupted.

"Yes…. Why do you sound like it's a bad thing?" Jordan asked cautiously waiting for his mother's response. She had tried to talk him out of going to the house, although he hadn't known why.

"Why did you not leave it for a few weeks like I asked? You know we wanted you to come and stay with us," his mother said with desperation in her voice.

"Mum. You know I just wanted to get out of London. I thought I told you that?"

"You did, but I thought you just wanted to get away from Sonya?"

"Mum, please don't mention that pathetic excuse for a females' name," Jordan pleaded. He remembered the woman that had stolen his heart, only to throw it back at him in pieces. With the help of his so called best friend of course. "Besides, I told you I was coming up here to get some writing done."

"Well, Sonya did give you material to work with," his mother teased lightly.

"That's not funny, you know I'm not a romance novelist," Jordan responded sharply.

"I know darling I'm sorry, I just couldn't help myself. So why didn't you go somewhere else for a few weeks first. Head up to Scotland or over to France and have some fun, before going to the house? They are just as lovely this time of year."

"Seriously mum… What's the big deal? I wanted to be on my own for a little while and felt like this is where I needed to be. So here I am." Jordan was starting to get a little frustrated with this subject of coming to the house against his mother's requests. "Mum…oh mother dear…. you still there?" he asked, noticing his mother's long silence on the phone.

"Yes I'm still here, sorry I just got lost in thought for a moment. I was just wondering……Do you still remember those silly stories my mum used to tell you when you were little?" she probed.

"The ones about other realms. The ones with elves, fairies, witch's and whatever else she could come up with?" Jordan asked.

"Yeah, those would be the ones," she replied.

"I remember some of them. Why?" he asked a little confused as to why his mother would bring this up now.

"No reason… Anyway I had better let you go so you can get settled in. No doubt, I will see you soon. Be safe, I love you my son," and with that she hung up.

Jordan looked at his phone. "Ok then," he said aloud to himself. His mother never ended a call like that. She must be getting senile in her old age, he thought. He grabbed his laptop bag from the back seat and got out of the car. He decided to head towards the boot to get the rest of his things, so he didn't have to come back out.

Once at the front door, he fumbled through his suit pocket for the keys. He looked at the beautiful red rose on the stained glass window imbedded in the front door and smiled to himself. He had always loved the design, even if it did seem that it wasn't as open as he remembered it to be. Not giving it another thought, he opened the door.

Looking around the entrance he always felt as if he'd stepped onto the set of 'Gone with the Wind'. The staircase and wooden floors had a beautiful shine to it. Jordan thought he could still smell a hint of polish. The crystal chandelier sent rainbows cascading over the entryway as the sun light shone through the open door hitting it in just the right places. He smiled to himself as he pictured his youngest sister sitting in the entrance wearing only her nappy, telling everyone about the 'pity ainbows'.

Jordan had always loved coming here and spending time with his grandparents. The house to him had always felt like home. His sister Jessica also loved spending time here, as did Charlotte. He never understood why his youngest sisters Janice and Joanne hated being here. Even Sonya had hated being at the house. She claimed she felt uncomfortable and never stopped complaining the whole time she was here. He would have thought being born at the house played a big part in their love for the place, except Charlotte hadn't been born here and loved it just as much as him. Jordan pondered that thought as he grabbed his cases and headed towards the stairs.

Chapter Five

Walking into the bedroom which had been his when he spent his summers here, he placed the last of his suitcases next to his bed and flicked the light on. He finally had a chance to look around. The room had changed completely since he was last here and guessed his grandparents redecorated not long before they died, since nobody went into their bedrooms at the burial.

No longer was it dark and dingy with heavy metal posters plastered all over the place. He smiled to himself thinking back to when he had first put them up. To him tight black jeans and black t-shirts with album covers on them were the best thing since sliced bread. Which went along with his long greasy hair to complete the look.

He couldn't believe how much he had changed. He had traded in his black jeans and t-shirts for an expensive grey suit and tie. Granted they were only worn to meetings with his publisher or editor. His long greasy hair was now long on top with short back and side's and a fringe that parted in the middle. His sister had said it reminded her of a hairstyle Johnny Depp had in one of his films, he couldn't remember for the life of him which one she said.

The bedroom had an elegant look to it. The walls were decorated with various shades of blue which had wood trimmings running along the edges. He liked it, as it reminded him of the bedroom he had shared with Sonya in their London flat. He smiled at the thought, knowing how much she had hated it. She hadn't cared much for the posters in the room either but he never had the desire to take them down even when she told him too repeatedly.

The only thing in the room that looked the same as he remembered was the freestanding mirror. The mirror looked like it was set in a gold plated frame which had a spiral design going all the way around. It stood at the foot of the bed by the wall and looked to be a few centuries old. Every bedroom in the house had an identical one. His mum had a large mirror in the lounge room sitting over the fireplace. It was the same design and looked just as old. He guessed she must have taken it with her when they moved down to London, not long after Jessica had been born. His dad had always carried a little compact mirror around that was identical to its larger counterparts. The only exception being the compact had gems on the case, which would occasionally flash. Jordan never could figure out how the gems flashed.

He decided to open the curtains to let in some natural light as he made his way around the bed towards the window. He stepped on the corner of the quilt draped over the bed, his other foot caught on the rest of the quilt corner and he stumbled heading straight for the antique mirror. Reaching out he managed to grab onto one of the bedposts to stop his fall. "That could have been dodgy," he mumbled to himself.

He really didn't fancy calling his mother to let her know he had smashed one of the mirrors. He could just imagine her, 'told you so,' comments. Opening the thick blue velvet curtains he looked out the window and saw the old oak tree. It was sitting in the middle of a beautifully mowed lawn. He decided that he would freshen up after his long drive from London, grab himself a coffee and enjoy the sunshine in the garden.

Chapter Six

Jordan stepped out onto the patio feeling clean and refreshed after his shower. It felt good to be in his blue jeans and his tight fitting white t-shirt. It seemed to mould to his naturally muscled frame, which always made the girls swoon. He never understood it himself, but he had to admit he loved the attention.

Taking a sip of his coffee, he snickered at the many memories of his sisters going mental at him. Their friends would be as Jessica had put it, having a perve session over him. *'Good times,'* he thought to himself. He looked through the door at the white jumper he had placed on the back of the chair in the kitchen. He had also picked up some daffodils for his grandparent's graves. He didn't know why out of all the jumpers he owned that one was the one he had brought with him. Its black swirly design screamed it wasn't the most masculine of jumpers.

Sitting down on the white cast iron chair, he couldn't believe how relaxed he felt. He loved the trips down memory lane he was having. He had very fond memories of this place. He looked over at the old oak tree and could picture himself with his sisters, sitting on a picnic blanket while their grandmother told them stories of other realms. He had always been amazed at how easily his grandmother would tell the stories and how real they had seemed when she told them. It surprised him that his grandmother's stories didn't inspire him to become a fantasy writer. His favourite story she told had been about a young prince who had been taken by his evil uncle. Closing his eyes, he let his mind drift back to memories of long ago that he has never forgotten.

"Because the evil uncle hurt the young prince, it sent out the call of the rose - "
"Nana Chris," A ten-year-old Charlotte said.

"Yes sweetheart," Christina, Jordan's grandmother replied.

"Is the call of the rose, like the rose on the front door?" she enquired.

"Yes, except this one is magical. It sends out a signal to all who are from the realm and calls them home," she explained patiently.

"So why has it been set off?" Jessica asked.

"Because the young prince is in mortal danger from his uncle. The call is summoning the Elf King back home."

"So he can save the prince?" An eight-year-old Janice said.

"Exactly my darling, so the Elf King can save his only son from his evil younger brother."

"How old is the elf prince Nana Chris?" Charlotte asked.

"Fifteen," she replied, glancing at Jordan briefly.

"You said he was fourteen last year," Charlotte protested.

"And every year you ask the same question. So why shouldn't he age as you do?"

"Yeah I guess," Charlotte said.

"Come on kids, let's go get some cucumber sandwiches and some fizzy pop. It must be lunch time by now," Christina said as she stood up from the grass where they had been sitting under the old oak tree. Gathering the blankets, she watched her grandchildren and Charlotte run back to the house.

Setting his coffee mug on the table Jordan smiled from the memory. He decided it was time for a reality check, as he needed to visit his grandparents' graves. At that moment it didn't feel like they were gone, it just seemed like they were out shopping or something. Making his way to the back door he reached to grab the flowers. He had deliberately picked daffodils, instead of roses. It was an inside joke for his Nan and the house being called Rose Manor.

When he reached the oak tree in the middle of the garden he spotted the two graves sitting under the horse chestnut trees. With a heavy heart he slowly made his way over to them.

Looking at the graves he couldn't help but notice how well maintained they were and wondered if there was a regular gardener that came by, that he didn't know about. Placing the flowers on both graves he kissed the tips of his fingers and placed them on the grave stones. He missed them very much. He smiled to himself when he decided that he would start writing down the old stories, as a tribute to his grandmother.

Returning to the table on the patio, he grabbed his coffee mug to take a swig and realised his cup was empty. He decided he would head back inside and get a refill.

Chapter Seven

When Jordan woke up he looked over the side of the bed to where his suitcases still sat. He really should have unpacked them at some point the day before, but he had decided to have a relaxing afternoon in the garden. Later that night he had watched the television and before he knew it, it was past midnight and he had gone straight to bed. He only stopped to fish out his sleeping attire.

"I really need to unpack those," he said out loud in the silence. He leaned over and grabbed his lap top from the top of his suitcases, where he had put it last night.

Placing it beside him he turned it on before pulling off the bed covers and slowly climbing out of bed. He put on his brown dressing gown and punched in his laptop password. He had chosen his sister's best friends name as his password. At the time he knew how much it would have pissed Sonya off. He knew she couldn't complain about it because otherwise he would know she had been trying to get into his computer. He still didn't know why he was with her for so long.

Deciding it was going to be a pyjama day, he went downstairs to have some food while his computer was loading up. He returned with a full stomach and a cup of coffee. He sat on the bed with his knees folded. Placing his lap top in front of him he began to type. He was actually quite surprised at how well he remembered the stories his Nan had told him.

After writing for a few hours he decided to stretch his legs and freshen up a bit, so he turned off his laptop, climbed over the other side of the bed, and headed towards the bathroom.

Jordan emerged some time later clean shaven. He was still in his dressing gown, which was open and revealed his blue and white striped pyjama bottoms and white singlet. The dressing gown belt was dangling by his feet. He shrugged at his attire and picked up his mobile phone and placed it in his pocket.

Dinner time he thought to himself as he started making his way around the bed towards the door. He hadn't realised how long he'd spent writing. He didn't notice his dressing gown belt had gotten caught on something and he tripped over it. Realising he was heading straight for the mirror again he tried to grab onto something, anything to stop his fall.

'Oh Shit,' Jordan thought as he braced himself for the collision.

Chapter Eight

Trixie walked into the elegantly decorated bedroom that would be occupied by her nephew for a few days when he arrived. Lots of greens and golds caught her eye and she could only imagine what his room looked like in the human realm. A shiver of excitement went through her at the thought of the human realm. She couldn't wait to see him and her big brother. It had been way too long.

With clipboard in hand Trixie made her way around the room, checking off things that had been done. She made her way around the bed to the elegant mirror and she touched the glass. She watched as the screen shimmered when she did a zig-zag motion over the glass with the tip of her finger. She couldn't help smiling at her reflection as it was further proof that her nephew was due to arrive.

She couldn't wait to see her nephew Jordan. She hadn't seen him in years. The only time she had visited the human realm was when Jordan and his sisters had been born and she highly doubted he would remember her at all, never mind remember she was his aunt.

The last time she had stepped foot in the human realm was when Joanne was born. Jordan would have been ten years old at the time and even though he would've been old enough to remember her, he was more bothered about his computer games or playing with Jessica and her little blonde friend. He didn't seem to notice the strange woman who stayed for the weekend and was effectively not seen again.

Ticking the last item on her check list she decided to go and have a little look at the room for her brother Richard. She didn't need to. The house knew what the King of Elves liked. She was just so excited to see her brother again and couldn't help herself. "Only a few more weeks," she said aloud while making her way back to the bedroom door. She hugged the clipboard to her chest in excited anticipation.

A loud buzzing noise suddenly started coming from the mirror and she halted in her steps. She knew it shouldn't be doing that so she slowly spun around on her heels, to see what was causing the noise. Trixie could only watch in horror as the young man she knew to be her nephew came crashing through the mirror and landed with a loud thud on the floor. It only took her a few seconds to realise that Jordan had somehow fallen through the portal and he was on his own.

"This can't be good," she said aloud as she leaned against the door frame. She placed her clipboard on the dresser next to the door as she did so. Not really knowing what else she should do, she decided to keep quiet and watch.

Feeling the pain in his arm and shoulder from hitting the floor, Jordan laid still. He kept his eyes tightly shut as he waited to be showered in broken glass. He was sure to hit the mirror and smash it against the wall with his weight.

When no glass fell, he slowly opened his eyes. He looked around on the floor and noticed that there wasn't in fact any shards of broken mirror and no blood from cuts he should have received. "What the hell," he whispered aloud.

Suddenly realising he was no longer in *his* bedroom, he glanced cautiously over his shoulder and had to do a double take to make sure what he saw was real. There was an old mirror identical to the one in his room and it was perfectly intact. He laid frozen to the spot paralysed with fear. He just couldn't seem to get his body to move. His brain on the other hand was going ninety to the dozen. Where was he? What was going on? So many thoughts bombarded his mind at once. He had to calm himself down somehow before he had a panic attack, which he wasn't prone to having. Concentrating on his breathing

Jordan could feel his emotions calming down but his body hadn't quite caught up yet, his fear still keeping him frozen.

Using only his eyes, he glanced at his surroundings. He was trying to get a clue as to where he was. After a few minutes, he came to the realisation that he couldn't see a lot from where he was on the floor, especially with the bed in the way. The frustration he was feeling was slowly replacing his fear. He decided he was having a bizarre dream after being knocked out from his fall, so he shifted his body and sat up. Looking into the mirror he noticed that the room seemed to be decorated identical to his, only it was green where his had been blue. Even the furnishings were the same except they were placed in different positions around the room.

Suddenly overwhelmed with curiosity, he slowly stood up and placed his hand on the mirror. Hearing a woman's voice chime from behind him, he froze. It was only now occurring to him that he could be in someone else's bedroom. He spun around quickly on his heels to face the source of the voice and stopped dead in his tracks, not quite believing what he was seeing.

Chapter Nine

There standing by the door leaning against the wall with her arms folded across her chest, was what looked like a tall pixie. She looked as though she had mugged Peter Pan for his clothes. '*Finding Never Land,*' he thought, suddenly remembering the film. He couldn't take his eyes off her it was as if he was mesmerized by her beauty. Even with her pointy ears and silver almond shaped eyes.

Realising he didn't see her in the mirror he asked, "How long have you been there?" He was clearly more concerned with his embarrassment than any danger he may be in.

"Long enough to see you're not so grand entrance," she said smiling at him.

"Oh," he said turning a bright shade of red.

"Don't worry, your secret is safe with me," she replied as she pushed herself away from the wall. "So what brings you here?" she asked looking him up and down. "I take it you don't usually travel in your sleeping attire?"

Looking down at his clothes he shrugged. "My attire is perfectly suited to the dream I'm currently having. If by some bizarre twist of fate, I happen not to be dreaming, I think my attire would be the least of my worries."

"Good point... however you're definitely not dreaming," she replied.

"A dream would say that even if they are…." He surmised. "What are you? A pixie or something."

"Are you always this forward with personal questions, I don't even know who you are," she lied.

"Oh…I'm Jordan Elfin," he said as he walked towards the woman, holding out his hand. "I do apologise…I have never seen anything or I mean, anyone like you before… in the flesh anyway." Dream or not there was no need for rudeness. Shaking her hand, he asked "So…. are you a pixie?"

"It has to be the hair. The short spiky look makes everyone think I'm a pixie." Looking at him she realised he seriously thought he was dreaming. His eyes looked like they were glazed over. How was she going to convince him he wasn't in fact dreaming? Not really knowing what action to take she answered his question. "I'm actually an elf…. I take it you haven't seen an elf in their natural form before?"

"Only in books…. My nan used to tell me stories about them when I was little," he said feeling like a complete prat once the words were out of his mouth. Changing the subject quickly he added "And, I'm awfully sorry to have appeared in your room like I did."

"It's not my room," she said blankly.

"It's not?" Jordan asked as fear started to take hold again.

"No I was just preparing it for our guest, who *should* have been arriving in a few weeks," she said casually.

"Are you a maid or something?" he asked.

"If you like," she replied trying to avoid the questions asked. She wasn't sure how to answer it anyway. "So what do you think?"

"It's very elegant, I have a room decorated exactly the same in blue, except for the tassels on the bed curtains," Jordan said scrunching up his face.

"Don't you like the tassels?" Trixie asked confused since the room should be exactly how he liked it.

"I can't stand them, but I'm sure your guest will love it," Jordan replied. This dream he was having was really bizarre. A pixie looking elf, what would he come up with next a fire breathing dragon?

"Hopefully he will," Trixie answered in confusion. "So do you still think your dreaming?" she asked changing the subject before she could dwell on the realms error.

"Hell yeah," he said in response.

Thinking of a way to prove to him he wasn't dreaming she remembered his grandmother was Christina of the Fae. Maybe if he saw her, he would believe it was real. "What if you spoke to your grandmother? The one who told you the stories," she asked.

"Then I would know I was dreaming."

Trixie looked at him puzzled. "How so?"

"My grandmother died a year or so ago, along with my grandfather," Jordan said sadly. He still missed them very much.

"Oh…I'm sorry for your loss. How did they die?" she asked sincerely confused.

"I don't actually know," Jordan answered. His mother was good at avoiding that subject. "All my mother would say was they were in a better place and not to worry about things like that."

"Ok, what about talking to your mother?" Trixie said not knowing what else to say.

He pulled his phone out of his pocket and looked at it. "Couldn't even if I wanted too."

"Why?" she asked.

"No signal," he replied placing it back in his pocket.

"I tell you what, how about we get you something to eat?" she said. She heard the rumbling sound coming from his stomach. "And when you're done, I will show you a much better way of communicating with someone other than using those silly phone things," she said taking his arm and leading him out of the room.

Chapter Ten

Jordan sat in a large dining room, enjoying the plate of bacon and eggs the pixie looking elf had brought to him. He looked around at his surroundings and couldn't help the thoughts that kept running threw his mind. Was *he* dreaming? The large dining room looked like something straight out of Hogwarts, so he figured he could be.

Was he going insane? He didn't think insanity ran in his family, although with some of his grandmother's story's it could be possible. Or maybe his split with Sonya did more damage to his mental stability than he realised. Maybe it was a strange coincidence the stories from his childhood just happened to be true.

Pushing all thoughts from his mind especially the last one, he turned his attention back to the woman in front of him and noticed she was smiling at him.

"So Jordan, you never mentioned how exactly it was that you got here?" she said. She was trying to make small talk while pouring two mugs of coffee from the pot on the table.

How did he get here? He was trying to remember the events of that day. His eyes widened in disbelief. "That can't be possible," he whispered mostly to himself. A feeling of unease was slowly creeping into his gut.

"What can't be possible?" she asked.

"Falling through a mirror," he answered. He could vaguely recall literally falling through the old antique mirror in his room.

"So tell me, why would that not be possible?" she asked, trying to get him to realise this was in fact really happening to him. He was in shock and she had to bring him out of it somehow before his skin colouring became even paler. If that was even possible.

Jordan looked at the woman like she had grown a second head. He didn't understand why she would ask such a question. "A mirror is a sheet of glass that is coated on one side with metal. A person cannot walk through glass. Never mind fall through a sheet of it without it smashing and cutting the person to ribbons," he said with a hint of sarcasm.

"Well you are currently sitting opposite an elf, so you could consider that anything is possible," she said smiling at him.

"Well since this is a dream and a bizarre one, I guess anything is possible when it comes to dreams."

"Ok then." It wasn't quite what Trixie was going for. "How about you tell me what happened, while you finish your coffee……refill?" she asked picking up the pot. With a nod of his head, she poured.

Sarcasm, finally an emotion she could deal with. Sitting back in her chair, she listened to how her nephew came to be in the neutral realm earlier than he should have been. She watched in sadness as the reality of his situation started to sink in. She felt the fear and panic radiating off him which was made stronger by the natural powers he didn't know he had. She wanted to wrap him in her arms and tell him she was his aunt and reassure him that everything would be alright. Trixie was surprised at the anger she felt towards her eldest brother for not having his son prepared for this major life change. She didn't want to cause him any more confusion so she said nothing.

"How is that for a crazy story," Jordan said while finishing the last of his coffee.

"And you told it so well…You should be a writer," she replied. She already knew he was one, hell she owned all the books he had written.

"I am," Jordan responded proudly.

"That will make it easier to write then," she said while standing. "I think it's time I showed you that cool communication device I mentioned to you earlier."

"Ok," Jordan said while getting to his feet. "Who will I be calling?"

"Someone you need to speak to the most," she said as they made their way out of the dining room.

Chapter Eleven

Richard sat outside on the white cast iron chair of his garden patio set, trying to enjoy the late spring evening. Tapping his fingers on the table he waited for his hand held communication device to return to him.

"Bloody Jessica," he mumbled allowed. His knew his daughter had pinched it for a make-up compact. He always had to hold back his laughter when she called him to tell him she had lost it and didn't know how. He was yet to tell her that it automatically went back to him when he needed it. She could have it for weeks and then it was gone, sending his daughter into fits of panic. It always amused him she would forget that she had taken it without permission in the first place and she would always loose it.

He was starting to get slightly impatient with the fact his compact, for want of a better word had not materialised yet. Granted he could just use the one in the lounge room but figured if he knew his sister, his wife would be on it shortly.

Richard couldn't shift the feeling of dread coiling in his gut from the moment he felt his son go through to the neutral realm. It wasn't Jordan he was worried about. Richard knew his sister Trixie would look after him, until he returned. It was his brother Vincent's sudden unavailability that worried him and the fact nobody had seen him since the time Jordan had entered the neutral realm.

Even with his powers dimmed from being in the human realm he could still sense his brother. Unfortunately, with all his powers as the King of Elves he was no mind reader and all his instincts were screaming at him that something bad was going to happen.

His brother Vincent had attempted to take over as king within hours of Richard leaving the elven realm for his new home in the human realm. For twenty-five years his brother believed he ruled the land and even Richard's most trusted generals were doing as he ordered.

Richard had been around long enough to know that those who were greedy for power and had gotten a glimpse of it, only wanted more and would stop at nothing to obtain it. His brother had changed over the years from the kind and gentle elf he once was. His soul mate had died during the battle of the realms over a hundred years ago and it had left him jaded and bitter. He had learnt the hard way from battle to not head into it blind. He would bide his time now, to see how things progressed and hoped his gut was wrong.

A flashing of lights caught his attention as he looked down at his communicator which had finally made an appearance. The flashes indicated to him that his sister was calling so he opened the compact and answered it.

"Trixie," he said.

"Don't Trixie me, why aren't you here with Jordan?" she shouted.

"Where is Jordan now?" he asked calmly.

"In the communication booth talking to his mother obviously, since you're on here talking to me," she huffed.

"So I hear," he said hearing his son yelling and Isabella's raised voice. "Trixie have you seen Vincent?"

"No, I've been busy preparing for your arrival, why?"

"Nobody has been able to get a hold of him. I'll get Mattias to try and locate his whereabouts, I'll call you later."

"Okay but when are you getting here and what am I meant to do with Jordan until then?" Trixie asked.

"I will be there in a couple of days, as for Jordan, keep him occupied in the neutral realm"

"You do realise his powers are uncontrolled and are flowing from him like a beacon?"

"Hence why he stays in the neutral realm. He is to go nowhere else. I mean it Trixie, nowhere else."

"Got it boss," Trixie said giving him a mock salute.

"Cheeky cow. I'll talk to you later," he said while closing the compact and ending the call. He made a quick call to Mattias before going inside to join his wife in the lounge room.

Vincent sat on the window sill of his bedroom in the autumn elf castle, staring out into the dark forest. Dusk hadn't long fallen across his realm. He had fled the main elf castle the second he felt a surge of power cross over him. He thought it might have been his brother returning from the human realm. He didn't want a beating from his brother for the liberties he'd taken in taking his place as king. Vincent wasn't afraid of his brother, not by a long shot, but he wasn't stupid either. The Elf King was the most powerful of all elves but as far as Vincent was concerned he was the Elf King now. His brother had lost the position when he left to have his cosy family life in the human realm.

Even now he could feel the power rippling along his senses. It wasn't long after he returned to his own castle that he realised it was a new power and not that of his brother. He knew that power all too well.

Vincent hated the fact that his brother was returning to the realm. He should have been at the main elf castle making the ordered preparations for his brother and nephews arrival. The nephew he had never met. His brothers return was only meant to be for a short period of time. He had to introduce his son to the realm and inform him of his duties. Duties that he himself had been fulfilling since his brother had left for the human realm.

Vincent had ruled as king and loved the powerful feeling it gave him. He sure as hell didn't want to give it up to some mere spit of a man. He wanted to keep the position and until his nephew had been born Vincent was next in line to the thrown of the Elven kingdom. He would have been King if something untimely had happened to his brother.

Vincent started pacing in his bedroom chambers. He could feel the power and recognised the familiar family energy, which it emitted. He thought it odd that it didn't feel like his brother had returned. If that was the case, then his nephew was here unguarded and only had his sister for company. He could work with that, the last thing he wanted was the wrath of the Elf King upon his head. He had to be clever and plan his approach if he wanted to keep control. He had to gain more power. He tapped the gem encrusted ring on his finger and suddenly smiled. He knew exactly how to obtain more power and nobody would be the wiser. If he could befriend his nephew maybe he could become a major influence over him and he would be able to still be in control of the realm.

He decided he would go the neutral realm in the morning to *befriend* his nephew. He walked out the room, ignoring his communication mirror which was flashing. It was his brother calling.

Chapter Twelve

Jordan found himself in a small room with a chair in it. The room reminded him of a photo booth, just not as bright. Sitting down he looked into what was clearly a mirror as his reflection was staring back at him. He noticed that it was an antique one. One that looked exactly like the mirror that hung above the sink in the down stairs toilet at his grandparent's place.

Following what the pixie had told him to do and feeling like a complete idiot, he closed his eyes and cleared his thoughts. When he opened his eyes he couldn't believe what he was seeing, no longer was he looking into his own deep blue eyes. "Mum?"

"Hello darling," his mother answered.

"What the hell?" He couldn't believe he was looking at his mother and could hear her quite clearly. How the hell did this thing work he wondered? He examined around the edges before looking back at his mother?

"What! I told you I would be seeing you soon," she said with a smirk.

"You also told me to be safe and I thought you meant face to face in the flesh not through a bloody mirror," he replied. He was slightly frustrated at how casual his mother was being, like this was nothing new to her. The penny suddenly dropped, "Mother......Where the hell am I?"

"Yeah, about that..." Jordan's mother started, wishing her husband was there to explain things. "You're in another realm," she finished rather quickly.

"Come again," Jordan said not quite sure if he heard correctly.

"You're in another realm," his mother said again a little slower this time.

"I'M WHAT!" Jordan said standing up abruptly and knocking the chair against the wall. He no longer believed he was dreaming.

"Jordan darling you seem to be freaking out a bit there. You need to calm down," she said in a calm voice.

"OF COURSE I'M FREAKING OUT, I MEAN BLOODY HELL WOMAN," Jordan shouted in a panic, forgetting who he was talking to. "WHY THE HELL WOULDN'T I……"

"ENOUGH," roared his mother.

Jordan stood in front of the mirror stunned. Had his mother just yelled at him or did the tiny room make it seem like that. He regained his composure and sat back down, pulling the chair closer to the mirror. "I apologise Mum. I shouldn't have acted that way"

"And how were you meant to of acted, sweetheart," said his mother gentling her voice. "You have just been told that you are in another realm, by your mother, who is looking at you through a mirror. I wouldn't have expected you to behave any other way."

"Really," he said cocking his eyebrow, not entirely convinced.

"Ok fine, I was expecting a lot of bad language to come out of your mouth," she admitted.

"Sorry to disappoint."

"Oh shut up," she said noticing her sons attire. "Jordan, why are you in your pyjamas?"

"It would seem I fell through one of those old mirrors this evening. While I was on my way to get some dinner," he said while blushing profusely.

"Dinner…. you're in your pyjamas."

"I decided to have a pyjama day. I spent most of my day in my bedroom typing up the stories Nan used to tell us."

"Ok… so how the hell did you manage to fall through the mirror?" his mother asked clearly amused.

"Is that really important?" he snapped. Softening his voice, he spoke the question which had been plaguing him. "How would that even be possible?"

"I don't know all the technical details about it, I never have. I do know that the old mirrors are portals to other realms," she replied.

"Portals to other realms?" he said remembering his grandmothers voice telling one of her stories.

"Well the neutral realm any way," she clarified.

"Neutral realm, you mean there are more," he said feeling his mouth go dry. He was starting to freak out again.

"That's where you are now and yes there are many other realms."

"So how did I manage to find my way here, falling through a bloody mirror? And why now? I must have bashed into those flipping mirrors a thousand times growing up and just hit glass, what makes now so special?"

"The portals were open as they were preparing for your arrival that's why you were able to fall through," his mother said lowering her head in shame. He should have been told this information long before now.

"My arrival?" Her words sank in and he suddenly realised what she was talking about. "You knew this was going to happen, that's why you tried to stop me going to the house."

"Yes and no," his mother said.

"What do you mean yes and no?" Jordan asked her feeling his frustration slowly bubble to the surface again.

"Yes I knew you were due to go, and no, I didn't know you would fall into the other realm. You are the first person to ever do that."

"Well lucky me, so how the hell do I get back?" he asked.

"You can't," she said.

"WHAT!!" he snapped.

"Not yet any way…. look I don't know the full details of the situation or how it works, I never have. What I do know is that you were destined to go through. It's kind of like being drafted I guess. My mother was trying to help get you ready for your time in our world and your father was meant to be preparing you for your role in it. So it wouldn't be such a shock to you." His mother tried to explain everything as best she could and cursed her husband for trying to get hold of his brother at a time like this.

"Nan's stories of course, now it makes sense why you asked me if I remembered them."

"What did you think, I was going senile?" she asked with a smile.

"Just a tad," he replied returning her smile. "Where is Dad?"

"He had some things to sort out, I will get him to contact you later…. Who told you how to use the mirror?"

"Some pixie looking elf, she didn't give me her name. I think she's a servant girl or something. Why?"

"Pixie looking elf," she said smiling, knowing it had to be his Aunt Trixie. "Well I imagine this servant girl has been helping you since you got there. When she comes back to get you just mention to her that you wish to use the mirror later to chat with your Dad."

"That sounds like you're going now," he whispered.

"I am sweetie but I will talk to you later, hang in their son. You will find out everything once you have talked to your father. I love you." With that parting comment, his reflection returned.

Jordan sat there in the silence thinking about everything his mother had said. He couldn't concentrate in the tiny room and was constantly fidgeting in the chair. A knock at the door brought him out of his thoughts and made him jump in the process. He opened the door to find the pixie looking elf standing there smiling.

"Hello," he said while looking down at her.

"So did you find out what you needed to know?"

"Not really, I have to talk to my Dad later."

"No problems, I can arrange that," she said looking at him. "Are you alright?"

"I don't know. I seem to be having trouble comprehending what my mother just told me and kind of dreading what my father will tell me. I'm just so confused. This still feels like a dream, but everything in me is telling me it's not. I just don't know what to think or how I feel at the moment," he told her honestly.

"How about I take you somewhere that will help you to gather your thoughts or better yet take you somewhere to let off some steam. You look like you could use a drink," she said taking his arm.

"I think I might just need one," he replied.

Chapter Thirteen

Jordan sat at an old oak table, in what looked like an old English pub with a pint of larger in his hand. He could have sworn he was in any old pub in London on Halloween. The different types of races around him were the product of fantasy in his world but here he was actually seeing it with his own eyes.

He knew there was an adjoining night club since he could hear the music loud and clear every time someone walked through the door. He had to admit it was a very tempting idea and he hoped the pixie looking lady took him in there.

"Thanks for the clothes," Jordan said to her making sure he spoke loud enough to get her attention.

"What?" Trixie said with a straw dangling from her mouth.

"The clothes…Thanks," Jordan said again as he pulled on the collar of the white shirt she had given him which was paired with a snug pair of blue stone washed jeans.

"Oh…your welcome" Trixie said as she turned back around to scan the small gathering crowd.

"So…umm," Jordan stammered. He had just realized the pixie looking elf still hadn't told him her name yet.

"Trixie," she said while turning in her chair to face her nephew.

"Trixie," Jordan said raising an eyebrow.

"It's actually Tracey, but only my parents and oldest brother can get away with calling me that. Speak of the devil," Trixie said as she pulled a gold gem covered compact out of her pocket.

"Hey Richard," Trixie said into the small mirror.

"Trixie, how is Jordan coping?" Richard asked from the mirror. Jordan perked up at the sound of his father's voice.

"He is dealing, want to talk to him?"

"Just a quick hello as I've got some business with Martouf to deal with. I know he is in good hands with you," he said. Trixie passed the mirror to Jordan. "Hello son."

"Dad, I've got so many questions and I don't even know where to start." He felt a little stupid for talking into a compact mirror.

"I know you do and I will answer them all in a few days' time when I arrive. I just can't right now, I have some urgent business to sort out in regards to the Elven realm…" and with that Richard was gone.

Jordan looked at the mirror, even more confused than ever. He handed the mirror back to Trixie and sat back in his chair downing the rest of his pint. "Elven realm," he muttered.

"That's just one of the realms. There are a few different realms," Trixie said. She wasn't very sure what Isabella had already told him.

"So, why is this realm called the neutral realm? It looks like it could be anywhere in London."

"One history lesson coming up," said Trixie as she signalled the bar man. After their drinks arrived and the waiter had left, Trixie began. "Basically the realms are mystical dimensions that do their own thing. Any supernatural being you can think of has its own realm. Not all realms intermingle with the other. The neutral realm just appeared one day…"

"How can a realm just appear?" Jordan asked incredulously.

"Let me finish," Trixie said in frustration. Trying to explain this was going to be hard enough without interruptions. So she decided on a different approach. "Do you believe in soul mates?"

"You're serious?" Jordan asked, taken aback by the random question.

"Very much so…so do you believe in soul mates?"

"Yeah."

"Good, that will make this easier to explain. When it became apparent that soul mates were not of the same race for example a witch and a Fae, the neutral realm came into being. Those whose soul mate was not of the same race would have somewhere to live and be happy, without having to be in a realm that was not their own."

"So where does the human realm come into this and our house?"

"There is more than one neutral realm, each of which is connected to the human realm and three other supernatural realms. Like this neutral realm is connected to the Elf, Fae and a Witch realm." Looking at Jordan's confused expression, she continued. "Think of it like the neutral realm is a square and on each edge of that square one of the other realms resides."

"You know maths and geometry aren't really my thing," Jordan said with a smirk.

"Oh come on, that was basic primary school stuff," huffed Trixie as she slouched back in her chair and folded her arms over her chest in defeat.

"I got it, don't worry you did very well at explaining. So do you know anyone who's had that happen to them?"

"What happen to them?"

"Their parents coming from different realms," Jordan replied.

Trixie sat there thinking for a moment, she knew a few people however she was pretty sure that Jordan had no idea he was related to them. Choosing her words carefully she continued. "Yes there was this one little girl, I used to baby sit every summer. Her mother was a princess of the Fae realm and her father was from the witch realm, one of them anyway. They actually lived in the human realm and every summer would come back here to do what they needed to. They stayed in the neutral realm and went to their realms during the day like a job. My oldest brother is also soul mated to someone who is not an elf and currently lives in the human realm."

"Who is your brother?" Jordan asked.

Smiling slyly, she figured she would avoid that subject and leave it to her brother to drop that bombshell on Jordan's head. "You will find that out soon enough…. Come on," she said while standing and grabbing her nephews hand from across the table.

"Where are we going?" he asked as he placed his finished pint on the table.

"The nightclub…. you have been eyeing it off all night," she said as she led him to the doors that joined to the nightclub.

Jordan once again could swear he was in any other London night-club. One that was from the disco era apparently. Mirror balls on the ceiling, light up glass dance floor and music from the seventy's and eighties. He couldn't quite believe other realms existed, never mind the fact they like to listen to the likes of Duran Duran and Earth, Wind and Fire to name a few.

Looking around the place he couldn't help but notice that everyone had stopped what they were doing and were looking at him. "What's everyone staring at?" Jordan whispered to Trixie, who was standing at his side.

Trixie looked back and forth between Jordan and the crowd. "New person in town," she said shrugging.

She knew that wasn't the case. It was the power he didn't know he had radiating off him in waves. Since he fell through the mirror the power flowing through him saturated the air around him. She couldn't help but worry over what type of attention he was getting but she knew he wouldn't come to any harm. Even from those who could feel his power and wanted it for themselves. She knew they wouldn't dare touch a hair on his head or they would risk the wrath of the Elf King. It was the ones who were checking him out, which had Trixie worrying the most.

"Move along people, haven't you ever seen a hunk in tight jeans before," Trixie said as she grabbed Jordan's hand and led him to the bar. She smirked at all the embarrassed faces that comment had conjured. Even Jordan seemed to have gotten embarrassed. Which only made her smirk wider.

"Did you have to say that," Jordan said once they reached the bar.

"Say what?" Trixie asked innocently.

"The hunk comment," he replied slightly annoyed.

"You mean you're not?" she said in jest, trying to get the barman's attention.

"Well I wouldn't say that," Jordan replied as Trixie handed him another pint.

"Modest much," Trixie said as she turned and leaned on the bar with her cocktail in hand. While sipping from the straw she watched quite a few females and males watching her nephew. "Jordan?"

"Yeah," he replied lifting his pint to his mouth with his back facing the crowd.

"Are you gay?" she asked loud enough for everyone to hear.

"No," he replied, almost choking on his pint.

"Single then?" she asked. She watched the smiles on the males faces turn to disappointment as they disappeared back into the crowd.

"Why?" Jordan asked her with raised eyebrows.

"You seem to have attracted the attention of some of the ladies, if that's what you would call them," Trixie replied.

"Okay then, well I'm not interested. I've not long come out of a long-term relationship," Jordan replied as he turned around to face the crowd. "Whoa, I wouldn't kick her out of bed."

"Who wouldn't you kick out of bed?" Trixie asked as she scanned the direction he was looking in.

"That bird in the red," Jordan replied. He couldn't seem to take his eyes off of the woman, like he was under a spell or something.

"Jordan you remember the way back to the house, don't you?" she asked recognising the woman in red. "You know just in case we get separated this evening."

"Yeah, but why would we get separated," he asked still unable to take his eyes off the woman in red.

"Good…oh look there's Lampros," she said as she took off into the crowd. Trixie knew the woman in red and noticed she had her sights set on Jordan. Trixie could do no more for him now and decided to leave him to his own devices and let his parents worry about the woman in red.

Chapter Fourteen

Ruby stood by one of the mirrored walls in a rather short, red, sleeveless, skin tight dress which left nothing to the imagination. If she wasn't worried about her breasts falling out the top then it was the bottom half riding up to give everyone a view of what she had for breakfast. She was horny and on the prowl for a suitable candidate to fill her bed. However that didn't mean she wanted the goods on display before the candidate had been found.

Ruby wasn't an ugly woman to look at. In fact she was very beautiful and favoured long dresses which fell to the floor and a low cut neck line that showed some clevage. She didn't need to dress up to the nines to attract the attention of a bloke. Hell she could just click her fingers or cast a spell and she would have one begging at her feet. That bored her though, plus lust spells could be just as tricky as the love ones so she tended to avoid them like the plague. She preferred to target the ones who would resist her natural charms, it gave her more of a challenge.

Turning around to admire herself in the mirrored walls she cringed. Apart from her dress, her hair was a fiery red instead of her natural wavy jet black. It was styled in tight curls, like she had used a cork screw to curl her hair. She couldn't help but be reminded of Kylie Minogue in her Locomotion video clip. This was the last time she watched a human 80's music show while casting a glamour spell when getting dressed. The only thing about her outfit that didn't clash were her emerald green eyes, which stood out.

Checking her make-up one last time she stopped short of applying fresh lip stick as a wave of power washed over her. Turning in the direction of the power source she couldn't help notice the rather handsome young man standing with the Elf princess. Ruby also noticed the worried look on Trixie's face as everyone in the room stared at the young man.

She couldn't help but wonder who this handsome man was. There was a familiar look about him, but Ruby was certain she had never met him. However that didn't stop her from deciding that he was her target. She tracked Trixie with her gaze as she and the young man headed towards the bar. She smiled at the hunk comment. Trixie had always been the comical sort and liked to lighten the mood when her brothers made a situation tense.

Fluffing up her curls, she decided to head towards the handsome young man. He finally noticed her and hadn't taken his eyes off of her. He didn't even blink when Trixie left him at the bar and joined the crowd on the dance floor.

"Hi, fancy a drink?" Ruby asked the young man once she reached him.

"Sure, why not?" Jordan replied turning to face the bar again and finishing the last of his pint.

"What you having?" Ruby asked, refering to his empty glass.

"Honestly, I have no idea what they are. I have drunk about six of them and didn't bother to find out what the hell it was," he said feeling the affects of the alcohol kicking in.

"Anything will do I guess."

"No problems," Ruby said as she hailed the barman to order the drinks. "So you new in town?"

"Is it that obvious?" Jordan asked when the drinks arrived.

"Kind of, plus I am pretty sure I would have noticed you before," she said smiling. She took a mouthful of her drink while watching Jordan over the rim of her glass. "So how long have you known Trixie?"

"I only met her today, but I'm guessing you know her."

"Yeah, I've known Trixie a while."

"Oh, were you the little girl she used to baby sit?"

Ruby almost choked on her drink with that statement. "Do I look like Trixie baby sat me?"

"Sorry I don't know what I was thinking," Jordan replied slightly embarrassed.

"It's okay, I know how hard it is to tell someones age. I'm actually an old friend of her eldest brother. I do know the little girl you speak of though, I have not seen either of them in many years. So what brings you to the neutral realm?" Ruby asked changing the subject.

"I kind of stumbled across it, I'm sorry I didn't catch your name, I'm Jor-"

Ruby placed a finger over his lips to silence him and spoke in her most seductive voice. "How about we leave the names, and just be two strangers making each others acquaintance and see where the night takes us?"

Jordan eyed the woman suspiciously. It wasn't the first time a woman had said that to him in a night club and it usually meant they were out on the pull. Most of the time he would politely decline as he was with Sonya at the time. There was one week where they had split up and he took the offers. He ended up having more sex in that week than he had in the whole month.

"You on the pull?" Jordan decided to ask.

"On the what?" Ruby asked never hearing that expression before.

"You know....on the pull. Out for a shag. Trying to get laid. Looking to hook up for the night?"

"Your rather blunt aren't you."

"I figured I might as well lay all my cards on the table instead of beating around the bush....So are you?" Jordan asked cocking his eyebrow at her.

"Yes I was planing on seducing you into my bed or yours," she replied because she didn't think there was much point in lying about it now.

"Oh," Jordan replied totally gob smacked at her honesty.

"Soooo," Ruby asked while twirling her hair in her fingers.

"Soooooo.... what?" Jordan asked suspiciously.

"You up for it or what?" Ruby said smiling.

She smiled a smile so seductive that it almost knocked the wind out of him. What the hell was in that last drink. His gaze drank in every inch of her. She was gorgeous, curves in all the right places, a body that was clearly built for seduction. Only a complete idiot would refuse a woman such as this.

"My place or yours?" Jordan asked as his lips crashed down on hers.

Chapter Fifteen

Ruby's eyes widened as the handsome young man's lips crashed down on hers, she wasn't expecting that to happen. He had taken her totally by surprise. Very few men had done that in the whole of her two hundred years of existance. She opened her mouth under his sensuous onslaught and it didn't surprise her in the least when his tongue suddenly clashed with hers. She couldn't stop herself from raising her arms around his neck as he ran his hands down her back and cupped her arse.

"So," Jordan whispered as he slowly kissed along her jaw.

"So what…" Ruby murmured while tilting her neck.

"Your place or mine?" he asked placing kisses down her throat.

"Yours," she replied without even thinking about it. She was too busy enjoying her rising passion with every light kiss he placed along her throat. It was only when he stopped kissing her and grabbed her hand that the foggy mist clouding her mind cleared. "What are you doing?"

"Going to my place," he replied.

"How are we getting there?"

"Walking I guess," he said shrugging slightly.

"Wait I have a better idea," Ruby replied sensing this man had Fae powers as well as Elf ones. His heightened emotions must have brought them to the surface. She knew how to harness another's powers and since his were so out of control, she could work with that. She stepped closer to him and placed his arms around her waist. Looking up into his lust filled eyes she said, "Think of your place" and brought his lips back to hers.

Within the blink of an eye they had reached their destination. 'Thank god for those Fae powers,' Ruby thought as she grabbed for the young man who seemed to have lost his balance slightly during transit. "Never flashed before, I take it."

"Uh no," he replied still slightly dazed "How the hell did you do that?"

"I technically didn't." Noticing the blank expression on his face she continued "Are we, where we needed to be?"

"I suppose," he said looking around the room he had stumbled into earlier. He noticed the soft glow of various candles around the room. It wasn't quite what he had in mind but his mother had told him that he couldn't get back home right now.

Ruby noticed the sudden disappointment which engulfed his features and grabbed his face in her hands so she could speak to him eye to eye. "Hey….Just go with it and don't think about whatever it is that is causing you such disappointment."

"Your right," he said as he claimed her lips once again with more passion than before. He ran his hands up her neck grabbing her hair. He pulled her head backwards and demanded access to her mouth. The clashing of their tongues was insatiable as he slowly moved towards the bed.

Ruby could do nothing but allow him to lead her there, unbuttoning his shirt as she went. They stopped when she felt the edge of the bed against her calves. He didn't lay her down as she was expecting him too. Jordan continued to kiss her as his hands ran down her neck and over her shoulders to the back of her dress, slowly pulling the zip down. He kissed along her jaw and neck tilting her head as he went. She couldn't stop the moans from bubbling up in her throat with each feather light kiss he placed along it. He alternated between seductive kisses and nips of his teeth on her skin. The onslaught made her bite down on her bottom lip to try and contain the bolts of electricity shooting through her body with every sensual moment.

Ruby didn't know if he was usually this good at stirring so much desire and passion in a woman with just his lips or if the ability was enhanced because his powers weren't under control. At that moment though she couldn't help but envy the woman who was destined to be his soul mate. She was going to be one lucky son of a bitch, even more so because there would be love there. What they were sharing was just lust and meant nothing, but she was going to enjoy everything he offered her this night. For on this night only, he was hers.

A shiver of desire snapped her out of her thoughts. Her dress slowly slid down her body to the floor revealing her red lace underwear. While his eyes were taking his fill of her body she seductively ran her hands up his torso and grabbed the collar of his white shirt. She pulled him down to her lips and slowly pushed his shirt over his shoulders. She couldn't resist the overwhelming urge to kiss down his throat to his shoulders, nipping him with her teeth before placing a kiss on the spot, to take away the sting. She followed the trail down his sculpted chest until she found his nipple. She swirled her tongue around the stiff peak and the groan from his throat sent shockwaves of pleasure to her core. Ruby kissed his chest as she moved across to the other nipple and her hands slowly slid down his tight abs to unfasten his jeans.

Ruby pealed the jeans and underwear over his tight arse and freed him from their confines. She was taken by surprise as he grabbed her waist and lifted her to stand on the bed in front of him. Running his tongue along the edges of her lace bra he reached her nipple and sucked it into his mouth, bra and all. The rubbing of the lace added to the sensations she was feeling, sending waves of pleasure though her. He slowly sucked and licked her lace covered nipple, the wet material sticking to her body. Cupping her other breast in his hand he squeezed lightly before kneading her breast in his palm. Ever so slightly he rubbed his thumb across the top of her peaked nipple sending shivers down her spine and making her back arch in search of more.

She was so lost in desire that she hadn't even noticed his other hand reach around her back and unclasp her bra. Slipping the straps over her shoulders, he placed small but tender kisses over her breasts. Ruby ran her hands through his hair and used her long painted red nails to scrape his scalp until she reached the back of his head. Fisting a handful of hair she pulled his head away from her breasts and slammed her lips on his, their tongues clashing furiously. He grabbed her around the waist and pulled her close to his body as her legs automatically wrapped around him. She could feel his long length lightly touching her arse.

She couldn't contain her excitement as he slowly lowered her onto the bed. The passion of his kisses was ever increasing. She moved herself up the mattress and he ran his hand down the side of her body resting on her hip. Spreading her legs he placed himself on his knees between her thighs. His large length was a mere inches from her moist core. She couldn't stop herself from bucking her hips as he ran a finger along the edges of her lace knickers, sending bolts of electricity straight to her already aching core.

She didn't think she could wait anymore. The emotions flowing off of him were mixing with her own desire and it was sending her crazy. She just wanted to feel him inside her. She wanted to be brought to the ecstasy every thrust of his hips would bring. She wanted to feel his hard cock pounding into her. She was beyond wanting, she needed him. Her body screamed for the release he could give her.

"Please take me now," she groaned.

"Patience," he whispered, smiling at her.

Lifting up her legs he slowly started to pull her lace knickers down, lightly placing kisses along her legs where the lace had just been. He dropped the flimsy piece of fabric on the floor to join her dress and bra. He placed her ankles on his shoulders and slowly placed kisses along the inside of her leg. His hand ran down the outside of her leg which sent hot shivers to the place she wanted him the most. Her stomach tightened the closer he got to her centre and she couldn't stop opening her legs wider for him.

She loved the feel of his hands on her as he cupped her arse. His breath was hot on her sensitive flesh and she could feel his breathing increase as her core got closer to his lips. He lightly placed a kiss on her mound before running his tongue through her folds, tasting her and sending shockwaves through her body. All she wanted to do was grab him by his shoulders, spin them on the bed and impale herself on him.

She wanted to milk him with her body and dig her finger nails into his chest. Shivers of ecstasy ran through her at the thought.

Her body tightened as his finger circled her nub relentlessly. Slowly he inserted a finger into her core and pumped causing a delicious friction. He placed kisses just above her curls slowly making his way up to her navel. Swirling his tongue around her navel he placed a second finger into her moist core and pumped again. "So wet, so tight," he mumbled against her skin. She moaned with disappointment as he removed his fingers from her body, placing his hands on the bed on either side of her. Anticipation swelled in the pit of her stomach as he started moving himself up her body, until he was covering hers.

She could feel his hard length against the opening of her core so she spread her thighs wider to give him better access to the place she wanted him most. He slowly slid into her and her muscles tightened around him as he sank into her warm depths. A thousand different emotions hit her at once as he withdrew and thrust back in again. Her hips met his thrust for thrust which brought her closer to climax, one she doubted she would forget in a hurry.

She imagined him to be a slow passionate lover, however tonight he was anything but. Her moans mixed with his and filled the room. With every deep thrust he gave, she was brought closer and closer to ecstasy. White light flashed within her mind and her body shook all over as she reached her climax. Her muscles contracted and milked the seed from his body as he climaxed. When he withdrew from her he nipped at her lips, before rolling onto his back next to her. He wrapped his arms around her and pulled her closer to him. She could see the sweat of their body's glistening in the low candle light as their heavy breathing slowly returned to normal.

Ruby lay there in his arms with her head on his chest and she could hear his heart beat slowing as he drifted off to sleep. It was only then that she actually paid attention to her surroundings. She suddenly had a feeling she had been there before. Lifting her head off his chest she looked at the handsome young stranger and still thought he looked familiar, but for the life of her she couldn't think why.

Placing a light kiss on his chest she slowly eased off the bed trying not to disturb him. She made her way towards the windows on the other side of the bed, grabbing her clothes as she went. Pushing the heavy green velvet curtains aside she looked out into the night as she got dressed. A well lit garden came into view as she looked over the patio. The plush green grass and a cobbled stone path stopped at a beautiful marble fountain. She could see little cherubs riding on the backs of dolphins. The dolphins had water spurting from their mouths and the cherubs held roses in theirs.

Ruby froze, her dress came to a stop mid thigh. She knew that fountain but she hadn't seen it in many years, not since before the great war of realms. She remembered a meeting with other supernatural beings. This house had been chosen because it was protected by Tristan. He had been and still was, a powerful witch and his wife Christina an equally powerful Fae princess. The house belonged then and still did, to Christina's family.

Ruby spun her head around to look at the young man on the bed as a sudden realisation hit her. No wonder he looked so familiar, this was Isabella's ancestral home. Pulling her dress up the rest of the way, she slowly walked over to the bed and placed a kiss on his forehead and the blanket over his hips.

"Richard's going to kill me," she whispered before she fled the room.

Chapter Sixteen

Jordan stood in the middle of a hallway in what was clearly the upstairs of a London house. He knew exactly where he was, even if he had no idea how on earth he had gotten there. He was in his sisters' hallway and was wearing the same clothes he had been wearing at his sister's birthday party. Jordan loved the feel of the outfit, which was one of his favourites. Jeans, a white t-shirt as always and his favourite black leather jacket which he loved.

His memory was a bit hazy. He couldn't quite remember what he had done the night before or where he had gone for that matter. He was pretty sure that he hadn't gone out with his sisters and ended up back at Jessica and Charlotte's place.

Voices from the end of the hall caught his attention so he turned his body in that direction and realised they were coming from the bathroom. The door was open and there was more than one voice, all of which he recognised. Not one of them were singing, so he figured they were getting ready to go out.

Not wanting to disturb them, he quietly walked down the hall. He passed some family photos along the walls that the girls had on display. Being a family meant everything to them, as they were all very close. When he reached the bathroom door he casually leaned on the door frame and folded his arms across his broad chest. He didn't say a word as he watched Jessica, Janice and Charlotte finish getting ready.

At least two of the girls looked beautiful in the out-fits they had chosen to wear, clearly they were going clubbing. Jessica and Charlotte always dressed similar and it was always something straight out of the eighties and tonight was no exception. Charlotte with her teased blonde fringe and curls in a half-up, half-down hair style that usually consisted of way too much hair spray. She had on ripped blue jeans with a bright colourful blouse that had shoulder pads. The top showed off her cleavage and it was matched with a big belt tied around her size twelve waist.

Jessica was dressed in a similar fashion, except she wore black jeans with a black blouse that was decorated in sequins. The belt she wore was basic black leather with a shiny buckle. Her hair was not that much different from Charlottes in style. Her brown hair was down and styled with big curls. She had too much hair spray in the teased fringe and had added blonde high lights. Jordan couldn't help wonder when she had gotten them done.

Looking at his sister Janice he couldn't help the protective big brother instinct flaring to life. He had the urge to go and tell her to put some clothes on. She wore what looked like a cropped tank top that was way too skimpy for his liking. Her skirt, if you could call it that, looked like a large leather belt, she had topped off the outfit with black high heels, and fish net stockings that just made him want to scream at her. If that is what she was planning to wear it was no wonder she was at Jessica's place. Their father wouldn't even let her out of her bedroom dressed like that, never mind the house.

He felt bad that he hadn't announced he was there but he just couldn't help himself, it was something he had always done to his little sisters. He would sneak up and scare the crap out of them when they finally noticed he was there. Granted some of the conversations he would hear he could have done without. A brother doesn't want to hear about the blokes his little sisters fancy.

His eyes kept falling back to Charlotte and the sad look she had on her face. She was smiling but it didn't quite reach her eyes. He couldn't help but wonder what was wrong with her as Jessica's voice interrupted his thoughts.

"Charlotte. No," Jessica berated harshly.

"And why not?" Charlotte's voice was equally harsh. "It could be the only chance I have."

"I said no," Jessica replied while applying her mascara.

"You just don't want me to be happy," Charlotte said sadly as she applied her hot pink lipstick.

"Charlotte Louise Finnissy, you know damn well that's not true," Jessica replied as she put her mascara in her make up bag and turned to face her best friend.

"Then why won't you let me say anything to him?" Charlotte asked with pleading eyes.

"Because he has just come out of a long relationship with a total bitch of a woman. Would you really want to be rebound girl?"

"Well, no."

"There you go then."

"But I love him with my whole heart and soul."

"I know you do sweetie," Jessica said as she pulled Charlotte into a tight embrace. "And until he can see what everyone else can see, you will say nothing to him on the subject. Let fate takes its course and as much as it grosses me out to say it, he could very well be the one for you. It just isn't time yet," Jessica finished smiling at her friend. She placed a gem encrusted compact into her hand bag.

"Yuck, I'm going to get a drink," Janice scoffed as she went to leave the bathroom.

Jordan's heart raced as his sister walked right through him. Turning around he watched her head down the stairs and out of sight. When he turned back to the other two girls it occurred to him that he had no reflection in the mirror. Fear crawled its way up his throat almost choking him and he was paralysed to the spot. Then it increased when Charlotte and Jessica walked right through him.

Jordan's eyes flew open and his heart was beating so fast he thought it would beat right out of his chest. He had been dreaming, but it had been so real. Never in his life had he had a dream that was so vivid. A fresh wave of panic washed over him as he took in his surroundings. Events of the day before slowly crept into his consciousness and the incredible events of the night before.

He couldn't help the wave of embarrassment that overcame him when he realised he was naked under the green quilt cover. The worst thing about the whole thing was he couldn't even remember exactly what the woman looked like and all he could picture was a blurred Kylie Minogue look-a-like in red. It actually surprised him that he could recall having mind blowing sex but couldn't recall with who. On the odd occasion that he had indulged in one-night stands, he had always been able to recall what the woman had looked like the morning after.

He looked to the other side of the bed, not at all shocked to find it empty. Shrugging off the quilt he climbed out of the bed, grabbing the first articles of clothing he saw. He put his pyjama bottoms and singlet on and picked up his dressing gown as he headed towards the door to go and find Trixie.

Chapter Seventeen

Trixie sat at one of the tables in the large dining room finishing off her coffee while she waited for Jordan. The large oak doors opening caught her attention so she turned her head in that direction and spotted her brother Vincent entering the room.

"Vincent," she called out as she rose from her chair to meet him. "Where the hell have you been? Richard has been trying to get hold of you."

"Morning to you too Tracey," he replied.

"Trixie," she corrected. "Did you hear what I said, Richard has been trying to get a hold of you."

"I heard you and unlike you I don't bow down to his every whim," he smirked.

"But he's the King."

"True, but you know what else he is little sister?"

"What?" Trixie asked frowning at him.

"Our brother."

"Big brother and what has that got to do with anything, *nobody* has been able to get hold of you."

"Well I have been busy."

"Doing what?" she asked as she folded her arms over her chest.

"I do not answer to you and what I have been doing is none of yours or anyone else's business. You seem to keep forgetting that," he snapped.

"Whatever," she said waving her hand. She had heard this argument more times than she could count. "So what brings you here? You haven't stepped foot in the neutral realm in years."

"I'm here to see my nephew, to give him a gift."

"What gift?" she asked suspiciously.

"This gift," Vincent replied as he pulled out the black velvet box from the confines of his cloak.

Trixie's eyes widened. "That's not what I think it is, is it?"

"And what would that be?"

"That cursed necklace."

"That is just a silly family story, there is no truth in it, at all."

"Will you be giving him the ring that goes with it?" she asked noticing the ring on his right ring finger as it always was.

"No…. should I?" Vincent asked.

"Yes…it's part of a set after all," she replied. Tapping her index finger on her lips she continued. "Unless of course there is some truth to those silly family stories, as you put it."

"There is not and he isn't getting the ring…. our father gave me this."

"Daddy gave you the set because Richard refused it and yet you are willing to part with half of it."

"And your point being?"

"Why only part with the necklace, if memory serves from the family stories, the necklace is a …"

"You are so paranoid, or is it just me your always suspicious of. All I want to do is welcome our nephew and give him a gift that has been in our family for generations or are you the only family member he's allowed to meet?"

"He doesn't know I am related to him. I was waiting for Richard to get here to tell him that. It was purely accidental that I happen to have met him first."

"Well where is he?"

"Still in bed I imagine, he had a late night."

"Well I'm going to get him up" Vincent said as he spun on his heel heading towards the door. He didn't get the chance to move before Trixie was in front of him with her palm on his chest to stop his progress. Vincent looked down at his sister's hand before looking her in the eyes. "What the hell are you doing?"

"You can't go wake him up," she replied.

"And why the hell not?"

"You wouldn't like it if a total stranger walked into your room to wake you up."

Someone in the door way caught Vincent's attention and at first glance he thought it was his brother but looking closer he realised it wasn't. "I take it our nephew looks like Richard."

"Yes, just not as tall, but bigger built…. why?"

"Because I think he's already up dear sister," Vincent said as Trixie turned her head to look behind her.

Chapter Eighteen

Jordan stood in the doorway watching Trixie trying to hold back an elf trying to pass her. He couldn't make out what they were saying, but the guy had a long black cloak on. Jordan guessed by the man's attire he was a Harry Potter fan. His outfit screamed Professor Snape. He had shoulder length black hair and black clothing from what he could tell that wasn't being blocked by Trixie.

The guy made Jordan feel uneasy and even more so when he practically barged Trixie out of the way. He headed towards him with his hand out and Jordan guessed he wanted him to shake his hand, but he felt disinclined to do so.

"Jordan I presume," Vincent said with a smile on his face.

Jordan just looked at him with a cocked eyebrow and folded his arms over his chest. "Who wants to know?"

"My name is Vincent and I am a loyal subject," Vincent said taking a small bow. He cast Trixie a dirty look when she snorted at his statement.

"Loyal subject?" Jordan frowned at that statement guessing this elf wasn't all there upstairs. He watched Trixie walk towards the elf and whisper something to him. The elf cocked his eyebrow at her in what Jordan could only assume was frustration.

"I bring you a gift," he said after dragging his gaze from Trixie.

The black velvet box he held out contained what looked like a gem encrusted gold necklace that matched the thick gold ring the elf wore. It even had a ruby looking gem sitting on top of the thing. He couldn't help notice there was something familiar about the way the necklace was set in the gold. It wasn't a delicate chain suitable for a woman who loved jewellery. The necklace looked like it could be worn by either male or female, depending on the outfit they were wearing at the time.

"It's a family heirloom if you will," Vincent said smiling.

Raising both eyebrows at the man Jordan asked, "Whose family?"

"Why yours of course," Vincent said with a forced smile. Jordan didn't know why, but he seemed to be grovelling. Vincent had noticed Jordan's look when he had pushed his way past his sister and knew that in order for him to accept the necklace, he was going to have to grovel. Vincent desperately wanted to gain the power that was flowing from Jordan, so grovel he would do.

"And you have it…. Why?" Jordan asked, folding his arms over his chest.

"A discussion for another time…. Perhaps you should try the necklace on for good measure, to see how it suits you?" Vincent suggested to see if he would go for it.

"No," Jordan replied flatly.

"Why on earth not," Vincent asked in shock. He wasn't used to being told no and winced at how desperate that made him sound. He had to get some control over his desire for his power or he was going to blow any chance he had of getting it peacefully.

"Because I said no. It's a necklace and a girly looking one at that. What with the gold design and the ruby looking pendent hanging on the end of it. It reminds me of the borders that outline the mirrors in my Mother's house, which are old."

"I meant to say, sire…. Would you not accept the gift to be worn by your young lady?" This was so not working out how Vincent had planned.

"I don't have a lady, young or otherwise," Jordan replied flatly.

"What about that Sonya woman?" Trixie said from beside her brother.

"Sonya?" Jordan twisted his neck so fast he was surprised he hadn't hurt it. "How the hell would you know about her?"

"Umm well…" Trixie started, not really knowing how to answer him without giving too much away.

"Never mind," he said before looking back at Vincent. "As I said, there is no young lady so I will have to decline your gracious gift," he replied. He placed his palm over his heart and gave him a slight bow of his own.

"Very well," Vincent said snapping the lid of the velvet box closed. He turned on his heels and walked out of the large doors.

"That was a bit sudden," Jordan said. He couldn't ignore the intense feeling of dread creeping into his gut.

"Yes it was," Trixie said. She bit her lower lip, worry creasing her brow. She knew better than to trust her brother, especially after the dramatic exit. "Come on, let's go get some breakfast and not worry about it for now." With that she laced her arm in Jordan's and led him to the tables at the back of the room.

Chapter Nineteen

Vincent slammed the door of the second bedroom in the Autumn Elf castle. Pacing over to the window he threw the velvet box onto the small wooden bed that sat next to the wall. He looked out the arched shaped window that held no glass and could see the lush green grass of the castle grounds and the dark forest beyond. He slammed his fist on the large grey stone window sill and spun around to lean against it with his arms folded over his chest. Only then did he realise what room he was in. The small room hadn't changed since he was a child, even the patch work quilt was the same. The room was the one his father would send him to as a punishment. It had become a sanctuary for him, especially after Constance had died. Grunting to himself he realised he hadn't stepped foot in his main castle apartments since that fateful day, one hundred years ago.

He had to think of another way to get the necklace on his nephew and try not to do anything to him that would set off the call of the rose. The last thing he needed was his brother crashing his way into the castle.

Vincent started pacing the small room, he knew exactly where he had gone wrong with meeting his nephew. He should never have pushed his way past his sister. He actually would have been happy to slap her to the ground for getting in his way. It would have been fine apart from the fact that since she grew up with two older brothers she could certainly hold her own against him. If he had to chase her, there was no way he would catch her. Speed she had an abundance of, not even Richard could outrun her.

Vincent knew he wouldn't be able to get his nephew to come to the castle on his own and very much doubted he could get Trixie to talk him into it. He needed to give his nephew an extended invitation to the castle before his brother arrived. He also knew that he needed to have an advantage over his sister. Power wise they were evenly matched, seeing they had the same powers.

"That's it."

Vincent suddenly stopped pacing, having come up with a plan. Looking at the large hour glass, he knew he wouldn't have much time.

"I really need to update this room," he said aloud as he walked towards the large oak door.

"Lampros," Vincent yelled, noticing his general and childhood friend walking past the door.

"My lord," the tall man answered with a bow.

"Enough of that crap, get in here." Vincent spat grabbing the man's collar and pulling him into the small bedroom before releasing his grip.

"What the hell Vince," Lampros said while fixing up his dishevelled brown leather uniform.

"Do we have any Fae in the dungeon?" Vincent asked with a wicked gleam in his eyes.

"Yes," Lampros replied eyeing his friend suspiciously. "Why?"

"Power boost of course and I will need you to keep an eye on a guest who will be arriving shortly. Just as soon as I go pick him up."

"Power boost and a guest?" Lampros enquired cocking his eye brow. "You're going to take someone and will need a quick get-a-way, hence needing a Fae?"

"Fine, yes, that is exactly what I will be doing. Before I venture to the human realm…"

"THE HUMAN REALM?" Lampros shouted. "You hate that realm and only venture there under dire circumstances. Richard is there I might add. He will know you are there the millisecond you go through." Lampros couldn't help the satisfied feeling that washed over him at the glare his old friend gave him mentioning their King.

"Since his son is here he won't give it much thought as to why I am there. He will most likely think I'm on the pull and leave me be."

"You know for someone who hates that realm so much you seem to have picked up a lot of their sayings. You could have just said you were looking for someone to warm your bed tonight."

"Do you forget who my sister is and her love of the entertainment of that realm? Speaking of my sister, once my guest arrives she's not to be permitted into the castle"?

"So are you actually getting someone to fill your bed tonight?"

"What! No…. Well I am not actually planning on it but thinking about it, I might have to. Either way Trixie is to be kept out of the castle."

"Is that an order?" Lampros asked cocking his eye brow.

"Yes, general, it is."

"My lord, it will be done as ordered," he replied bowing slightly.

"Good. Now let's go get me that power boost," Vincent said rubbing his hands together as he headed out of the room. "Oh by the way I will need you to distract my sister, while I collect our guest."

"Yes my lord," Lampros replied glumly. He knew what was coming. Another Fae family were about to lose a loved one and once again Vincent was using his affections for Trixie against him. He really didn't know how much more he could take before he snapped, or worse, lost his soul mate.

Chapter Twenty

Jordan let Trixie lead him into a beautiful garden, similar to the one at his Mother's ancestral home. Had it been only yesterday that he had been there? He did notice a few subtle differences with the garden. Instead of the old oak tree, there was a beautiful water fountain. He made his way towards the fountain, with Trixie strolling next to him.

"Isn't it a beautiful afternoon," Trixie said trying to make conversation. "Did you not find the clothes I set out for you?"

"What?" said Jordan, not hearing what she said. His eyes were so fixed on looking at the dolphins and cherubs that made up the fountain and noticing all the trees that were along the edge of the garden, that his mind had drifted elsewhere for a moment.

"Your clothes? Didn't you find the jeans and tee-shirt that I put out for you?"

"I guess I didn't notice them," he replied in all honesty while looking down at his sleeping attire and the dressing gown he was wearing.

"Oi Trixie," a voice called from the back doors of the house. Trixie and Jordan spun their heads towards the sound.

"Lampros," Trixie whispered as she clasped her hands together.

"Who?"

Jordan noticed the way Trixie's eyes lit up the second she saw the Elf in front of them.

"Just a friend," she replied.

"Yeah sure."

"He is," she snapped indignantly.

"Better go see what he wants hey?" Jordan teased.

"Yeah I guess," Trixie said looking back at her nephew. "I think I will go and fish out those clothes for you as well while I'm at it."

"I'll wait here," Jordan replied as she walked off towards the house. He did hope that the clothes would fit since she hadn't asked his size. He hadn't realised how warm it was under the hot rays of the sun. He took off his dressing gown and threw it over his arm as he walked slowly around the fountain in the centre of the garden. The garden was surrounded by loads of trees instead of a high wall and it was putting Jordan on edge. He hoped Trixie would be back soon because looking into the trees that stretched for miles around the grounds was giving him a feeling of being watched and he didn't like it. The episode with that Vincent character this morning had unsettled his nerves a bit.

Movement from the trees caught his attention and his eyes locked on the area. He tried to look into the trees to see what could have caused the movement, since there was no breeze. His breath almost caught in his throat when he noticed a figure in black moving between them. He squinted his eyes trying to get a better look and was surprised when a bolt of lightning shot out of the trees, hitting him in the chest.

"What the hell," he said aloud before dropping his dressing gown. He didn't have time to register what had happened before a second bolt hit him. This bolt was stronger than the first and it knocked him out cold.

Chapter Twenty-One

Trixie walked out into the garden with Lampros and stopped dead in her tracks. Something was wrong she could feel it. She quickly looked around for her brother since she could still feel his presence. It could be a lingering residual feeling from when he was there that morning but she wasn't entirely convinced, so she decided to see where Jordan had gone.

Where had he gone she wondered? There really was only so many places a person could go in the garden, unless they ventured into the forest. She couldn't ease the feeling of dread that had taken residence in the pit of her stomach, so she slowly started walking towards the water fountain.

As she got closer she noticed what looked like a piece of clothing on the grass next to the fountain. With a surge of panic, she ran towards it and picked it up. She realised it was the dressing gown that Jordan had been wearing. It had a black scorch mark on it, that weren't there earlier. A hundred thoughts raced through her mind at the same time. *'He wouldn't, he couldn't, but I bet he bloody did.'*

"VINCENT," she screamed at the top of her lungs, hoping he wasn't too far away to hear her.

She had to think. *Had Vincent taken their nephew and if so what for? It would have to be for his power. Jordan doesn't know he has any and is therefore unable to defend himself.*

She had to make sure that Vincent had Jordan and what his purpose was for taking him. Before she could bolt into the trees after her brother someone caught her by the elbow.

"Trixie wait," Lampros said with guilt all over his face. The look of betrayal in her eyes broke his heart.

"You…. you were in on this," she said wrenching her arm out of his grip.

"Trixie it wasn't like that," he pleaded.

"Really!! So you weren't distracting me with your affections while my brother proves once again how low he has sunk by steeling our nephew?" Trixie tapped her foot and placed her hands on her hips waiting for him to say different.

"Okay so it was like that…But only because that was the only thing I could think of to distract you." His heart broke all over again at the look of hurt on her beautiful face, before she gave him a death glare which made him wince. Thank god that wasn't one of her actual powers.

"You are a liar and a betrayer and you can stay the hell away from me," she snapped turning her back on him.

"Trixie I only did what I was ordered to do."

"What, where you sent to distract me? Did my brother say, hey you love my sister can you use that on her while I take my nephew and steel his powers?"

"Trixie I do love you. I didn't even know who the person was that Vincent planned to take never mind for what purpose."

"Not only have you just proven how disloyal you are to everyone except Vincent, but you are clearly not to be trusted. *You* are still doing what was ordered and distracting me."

"Trixie," Lampros pleaded.

"I have a nephew to retrieve no thanks to you. So you can just kiss my arse and leave me the fuck alone."

Trixie couldn't help but feel hurt and betrayed as she watched Lampros walk back to the house with his head bent in shame. She had more important things to concentrate on like getting her nephew back and making sure her brother, had in fact taken him. She knew that if Jordan was in any life threatening danger, being of royal blood and next in line to the throne, the realm itself would summon back the king. Vincent knew it as well and was clearly being sneaky with obtaining Jordan's powers, if that was in fact his plan.

She had to concentrate now so she closed her eyes and focused on Jordan and his uncontrolled power. It would be the ticket to finding him and would be easier than trying to sense her brother. She could feel his presence in the neutral realm, so he hadn't been taken far. Running as fast as she could she headed in the direction she could sense her nephew was being taken in. Dodging trees and bushes at a speed no human could undertake she finally spotted an unconscious Jordan. He was draped over Vincent's shoulder in a fireman's lift.

She slowed her pace to a walk until she was mere meters from her brother. She stopped in her tracks as Vincent turned around and noticed her walking behind him. The grin Vincent had on his face gave Trixie the creeps but before she could even finish shuddering from the strange sensation, Vincent disappeared with Jordan in tow.

"Crap." She could no longer feel Jordan or Vincent in the neutral realm. "Where the hell has he taken him?" she muttered aloud.

Not knowing what action to take or what his intentions are she decided to consult an old friend before she told Richard and Isabella what had happened.

Chapter Twenty-Two

Trixie was kneeling in front of a large crystal looking throne a short time later. She hadn't been there in years as the place always reminded her of an ice palace.

"Your highness, I come seeking your guidance." She looked up into the blue eyes of an older woman with long white hair, which matched the dress she was wearing.

"Princess Tracey of the elves. What is it that would cause you to come to me for aide and not either of your brother's?" she asked.

"It is a matter that involves Vincent and I thought I would consult with you first since Richard is currently in the Human Realm."

The woman looked at Trixie before standing and heading towards her. She signalled Trixie to rise and the woman pulled her into a tight embrace, all formalities gone. "My god it's good to see you," the woman said.

"Same here," Trixie said as she pulled herself out of the embrace. "I just wish it were under better circumstances."

"Trixie, what is going on?" The woman asked placing her hands on her hips.

"Vincent has taken Jordan."

"What! My Jordan?" she asked with confusion.

"Yes."

"I don't understand. Jordan isn't due here for a few more weeks. How could *anyone* have him?"

How was she going to explain this? Briefly would be better, Trixie thought to herself. "Jordan went to the house too early and fell through his mirror."

"Fell through his mirror," the woman said bursting out laughing. "I shouldn't laugh."

"What. You never told him about that in the stories?" Trixie asked. The woman who Trixie was talking to was none other than Christina of the Fae and Jordan's grandmother.

"I never knew it could happen," she said sternly. "How do you know Vincent has taken Jordan?"

"I saw Vincent carrying Jordan over his shoulders. He gave me a grin that made me shudder and then he vanished."

"So the young prince has indeed been taken by his evil uncle, blast it!! Hang on, what do you mean Vincent vanished?" Christina asked in shock.

"Exactly what I said, he vanished…. like poof…. just disappeared before my very eyes."

"Elves don't have that ability, so how the hell did he accomplish that?"

"Vincent must be taking powers from others," Trixie surmised.

"That would explain why some of the Fae have gone missing."

"Missing?" Trixie asked confused.

"Yes. Not the most powerful ones amongst us, whose absence would have been easily noticed but others have just disappeared. We have found no trace of them," Christina whispered solemnly.

"How long has this been going on for?" Trixie asked.

"Honestly? Since Richard went to the human realm. I only found out about it when I came back. Considering what you have just informed me of, I think I can guess their fate."

"You think Vincent has killed those of the Fae that are missing?" Trixie asked not really wanting to hear the answer.

"What do you think?" Christina asked giving her a stern look. "Your brother has powers that he shouldn't have and Fae have just vanished without a trace. Question is not only how and why but what the hell does he want with my grandson if it's not to take his powers? It's not like he is a doting Uncle. He hasn't been himself since the Battle of the Realms."

"So what do we do?" Trixie asked with pleading eyes.

"I can't do anything until the King of the Elves requests it," Christina said regretfully.

"What!!" Trixie said shocked. "Why?"

"Trixie have you forgotten how the realms work? My grandson is the Prince of Elves, therefore only the King of the Elves can do anything. As soon as the call of the rose has been sent, *all* realms will shut off until they are needed. Anyone who is not in their own realm will be automatically flashed back. If it was one of his sisters that would be a different matter," she explained.

"How so?" Trixie asked totally confused.

"All I know is one of the girls is destined to come here and another one is to go to the realm of the witches. The last one is to be a guardian, however before you ask I don't know which one is going where. I will know that nearer to their twenty-fifth birthday's, when the realms start preparing for their arrival."

"So unless Richard requests for you to join him you are stuck. Is there no other way?" Trixie asked.

"If Richard was to fall in battle while trying to get Jordan back then Tristan and I would be called to take over his rescue."

"What about Isabella? Won't she get called along with you and her father?"

"I would say so, but what realm she will be in once she is called is any one's guess."

"You're making it sound like she won't be coming through with Richard."

"The house won't let her but if I know my daughter, as soon as the call of the rose eases and allows it, she will be through…. Maybe you should meet her when she gets here, you are her oldest friend."

"Oi," Trixie said slightly insulted.

Christina laughed. "I didn't mean it like that, you doughnut."

"Better not have, I know I have a hundred or so years on her, but you didn't have to point out the age difference."

"And yet my dear, you have always acted like you were in your twenties."

"I know right…. acting older is so boring."

Christina turned to Trixie with a serious look on her face. "So what are you going to do now? Inform Richard of what has happened?"

"Not yet…. Since Richard has not been summoned here we have to assume that Jordan is not in any life threatening danger. I will head off to the Elven realm and see if I can sense him there and try to find out what Vincent plans to do with him. I don't know what else to do," Trixie said with worry in her voice.

"Well my sweet at least you have a plan, that is a start. I now have the unfortunate job of informing Tristan that his grandson has been taken," Christina said with worry creasing her brow. Giving each other a farewell hug, they went their separate ways.

Chapter Twenty-Three

Vincent arrived in the bedroom of the Autumn elves castle and dumped his still unconscious nephew on the bed next to the wall. He started pacing the room thinking what his next move should be. Vincent clearly hadn't thought things all the way through. He really needed to control his lust for power, or at the very least learn to think before acting.

His attention was brought back to Jordan when he noticed him stirring. 'Crap,' Vincent thought. It was taking a lot of power to keep Jordan hidden from Trixie. He knew his sister would try and get Jordan back. The second bolt of lightning Vincent used to take down Jordan had almost wiped him out. He hadn't thought his nephew would be so powerful, which made him lust even more for the power he possessed.

He pushed what little power he could spare into Jordan to keep him unconscious. He needed a power boost but didn't want to risk forcefully taking Jordan's power. He didn't know what effect it would have. He realised that he had stopped pacing and was tapping his golden gemmed ring. He suddenly remembered the other half of the set and headed to his night stand. He opened the top draw and a rush of panic went through him. The box was gone. Glancing over the room he spotted the black velvet box under his nephew's forearm. With his haste that morning he'd forgotten he hadn't put the box back in its proper place.

He picked up the box and slowly opened it revealing the thick gold gemmed necklace, it cast a slight glow around the small room. This was just what he needed. Taking the necklace out of the box he lifted Jordan's head slowly as not to wake him. He carefully placed the heavy chain around his neck. Vincent could feel the power draining from his nephew and passing into him almost instantly.

He was indeed very powerful, almost as powerful as his father. Vincent couldn't help the evil grin that spread across his face. With Jordan's power and his own he might have enough to overthrow his brother and take the throne. If Jordan was out of the picture as well he would be the next in line to the throne. He would have to make sure Jordan was out of the reach of his sister. Vincent knew that Trixie would come after Jordan and she would look here first. He couldn't keep him shielded forever, not even with Jordan's power to boost his own. The necklace would keep him unconscious for now. He decided to send one of his guards to go and find Lampros, while he got ready for his trip to the Human Realm.

A short while later Vincent stood in the middle of the room facing the window in a very expensive suit and tie. His hair was tied back in a low pony-tail and his nephew was still out cold on the bed. He turned at the sound of his bedroom door opening. "Lampros."

"Don't you Lampros me, you wanker," the other Elf replied as he marched up to Vincent.

"I take it things with my sister aren't going so well," Vincent said adjusting his black silk tie.

"Aren't going so well, she isn't even fucking talking to me because of you. In fact, she wants nothing to do with me," he seethed.

"And why is that my fault?" he asked calmly.

"Oh, I don't know. Might have something to do with you ordering me to distract her while you nicked off with your nephew," Lampros replied waving his arms in frustration.

"And how exactly did you distract my sister?" Vincent asked raising his eyebrows. If it was any other guard talking to him like that, he would have disposed of them without a second thought.

"That doesn't matter," Lampros replied sheepishly.

"Lampros. If you used your affections for my sister as a distraction and it bit you in the arse, that is not and I repeat *not* my problem."

"You fucking Cu…"

"HAVE YOU FINALLY FINISHED?" roared Vincent glaring at his old friend.

"Not by a long shot," spat Lampros, glaring back.

"Tough. You are the head general of my elves and you will show me some respect as your king," he snapped. Vincent had grown tired of his friend's emotional ranting and Lampros' snort didn't go unnoticed either. Vincent had more important things to deal with right now. He needed to leave for the human realm to put the next part of his plan into action and he needed his general. An emotionally wounded friend, he really didn't want to deal with right now.

"Now I need you to keep my sister out of the castle," Vincent said. He turned around to fetch the bottle of aftershave from his top dresser draw and placed some on his clean shaven face. He turned to see Lampros glaring daggers at him. "Don't look at me like that."

"I don't fucking believe you!!! After what I just told you, you are still expecting me to keep her out of the castle?"

"No, I am expecting you to do your job and follow my orders. The fact that she is not talking to you would make that task much easier for you, I imagine. Besides who said *you* personally have to do it," Vincent said raising his eyebrow at his friend. "Place guards all around the castle if you must."

"Is it really that important that she stays out of the castle?"

"Yes. She will be coming to get our nephew and I'm not ready to give him up yet."

"You have never forbidden her from the castle before. If she's persistent what would you have me do, kill her? Just to keep her away from your nephew?" asked Lampros raising an eyebrow at Vincent and folding his arms over his broad chest.

"Kill her?" Vincent said. He was shocked that his friend would even come out with that. "You of all people wouldn't touch a hair on her head. You would sooner kill me than her. No. I just need her to stay away from here. Once I leave for the human realm, my nephew will no longer be shielded from her. She will be very persistent, so you or one of the other guards will have to keep Trixie distracted…. and *THAT* is an order," Vincent said with formality in his voice.

"As you say my lord," said Lampros bowing in formality before turning and heading towards the door.

"Oh and Lampros," Vincent called to his friend who turned to look at him as he reached the door. "Try not to kill any other elves that try to distract my sister, hmmm?"

"Can't promise you that my lord," he muttered and without another word the elf was gone.

Vincent looked over at his nephew while adding solid gold cuff links to his attire. He needed to make sure nobody entered the room in his absence. Opening the door, he looked at the two guards standing there.

"Nobody is to enter this room except for me. Anyone who tries to, kill them."

"Yes my lord," said the two Elves in unison as Vincent closed and locked the door.

Chapter Twenty-Four

Trixie returned to the Elven realm after finding no trace of Jordan. She headed towards the autumn elves castle her brother Vincent resided in. To her surprise and relief, she sensed Jordan's presence. She guessed Vincent had been shielding Jordan from her somehow and it put her on edge that he wasn't anymore. Trixie wasn't a warrior but she wasn't stupid either. She knew her brother would have taken measures to stop her getting to Jordan. Why hadn't she just asked Richard to come back here. She quickly put that thought out of her mind and quickened her pace towards the dark forest which led to the Autumn Elves castle. This was the only area, in any kingdom, that Vincent did actually have authority in.

When she reached the end of the dark forest that lay just beyond the castle, she noticed that there was an unusual amount of guards posted everywhere. Trixie had no doubt they had been placed there to stop her getting in. She was going to have to be sneaky and since she was a female she could use that to her advantage. Reaching into the leather purse attached to her belt she pulled out her compact communicator to use as a mirror. She has a special lip-stick with her that she had a witch friend make for her. Trixie put the lipstick on. It was currently a bright red, but it would change colour to attract whoever she planned to render unconscious after a small kiss. Smacking her lips at her reflection, she closed her compact mirror and placed it back in her purse. It wasn't really a purse as it looked more like a bum bag from the eighties, but she didn't care.

Trying to act like it was a normal day she walked casually along the long stone path toward the castle. Her hands were behind her back as she took in the scenery that she had seen hundreds of times before.

The grass on either side of the cobbled path was as lush green as always. She could even hear birds singing as the sun beat down on her. It really was a beautiful afternoon.

She reached the main gates and stopped abruptly as one of the guards stood in front of her. "Why do you block my path?" she asked the elf in front of her.

The elf smiled at her. "I'm sorry Princess, but we are under orders not to let you pass."

"Is that so and under whose authority?" she asked.

"General Lampros, Princess," the elf replied.

Trixie stepped back slightly shocked, she hadn't seen that one coming. How was she going to deal with the situation now? Her lipstick would be pointless, having more than one guard present. The other would raise the alarm, before she could even get near him. There was only one thing for it. "I wish to speak to him." The elf just looked at her.

"NOW," she said with authority, while discreetly waving her fingers at him Star Wars style. Being Princess of the Elven realm gave her some authority and certain benefits. However, she couldn't over rule either of her brother's.

"As you wish." The elf turned closing the main gate behind him leaving Trixie there.

"Bloody cheek," she muttered aloud tapping her foot with her hands on her hips, waiting for him to return.

After a few minutes the elf returned with the General. Trixie stared into the dark green eyes that were Lampros'. She always melted every time she looked into them. God he is gorgeous, she thought. The sound of someone clearing their throat brought her out of her stupor. Pulling herself back together she turned her attention to Lampros acting like she hadn't just been drooling over him. After all she was still mad at him, wasn't she? The big grin on his face told her he had noticed her gawking.

"Trixie," Lampros said nodding his head at her.

"Lampros, why are you not letting me into the castle?"

"Vincent has given his orders," Lampros said sternly.

"Oh has he, well I want to see my brother. NOW," Trixie said using the same trick as she had before.

"Trixie, I am not as weak minded as this idiot," Lampros said nodding his head in the direction of the other elf as he folded his arms over his toned chest. "That little trick won't work on me, nor do you have the authority."

Trixie looked at Lampros. She knew getting past him wasn't going to be easy and the direct approach clearly wasn't working. Suddenly remembering the lipstick, she looked at Lampros with a sly smile and then looked at the other elf. She could use the lipstick on Lampros but he would have to be alone because she didn't fancy trying to seduce him with an audience. Plus, if she kissed him and he passed out the alarm would be raised. She knew Lampros had feelings for her and didn't really want to use that against him, but she had to get to her nephew. God only knew what Vincent intended to do to Jordan and since he wasn't allowing her into the castle she figured it couldn't be good. Even though she couldn't actually sense her brother in the castle.

"Ok then," she suddenly said.

"What?" Lampros said surprised.

"Well, Vincent must be really busy with something. I will go, but please inform my brother that I stopped by," she said with a big smile on her face.

"That's it?" Lampros said pinning her with a suspicious glare. "You're not going to kick up a stink or anything like that?"

"Lampros darling, you should know me better than that," she said smiling sweetly at him.

Now he was suspicious. He did know her which is why he knew she had to be up to something. He was curious so he decided he would leave it be for now and see what she was planning to do.

"Well on that note milady, I shall bid you a good day," Lampros replied bowing low. He turned and walked back through the gate and headed straight to his room. From there he had a good view of the castle grounds and could watch her without being seen.

Trixie bowed and smiled in return. After Lampros closed the gate behind him, she turned on her heels and headed away from the castle. She was trying to give everyone the impression she was leaving. She knew Lampros wouldn't have gotten very far so she headed back to the dark forest. She would have to wait a little while before heading back to the castle.

Chapter Twenty-Five

Vincent made his way to the portal at the edge of the Elven Realm. He had taken a brisk walk trying to conserve what power he'd acquired from his nephew for the mortal realm. He knew his power was dangerously low and he wanted to conserve it so he could flash to his nephews flat. He had to find out as much information as he could about this Sonya woman so he could bring her back to the Elven Realm.

Once he had tracked her down and brought her back, he didn't quite know what he was going to do with her. He didn't even know how he would get her to the realm without her noticing. All this effort so he didn't accidently send out the call and force his brother to come back. He was normally very calculating with his plans but at the moment he just seemed to be winging it. He hadn't expected his nephew to suddenly turn up without his brother, let alone with uncontrolled powers. He had no plan in place to take the powers because his plan with the necklace had fallen through. Unfortunately, he made the mistake of barging his way past his sister and almost sending her flying. His nephew didn't seem to appreciate that. Maybe he could use that knowledge to his advantage when this Sonya woman was involved.

Stepping through the portal Vincent emerged on the other side in what looked like dirty alley, a small one at that. There was barely enough space to walk through it especially with the rubbish bins lined along the walls. He had to admit the bins were all in a nice neat row, even if the lids were not down as they should be. The buildings were separated by about two meters of pavement, if that. He wasn't exactly a doting Uncle, but he sure as hell hoped none of his family lived in this place.

Vincent closed his eyes, he didn't want to risk walking through the alley and stepping on anything in his expensive shoes. He pictured his nephew in his mind and thought of being at his flat, harnessing his power and flashed from the alley.

Opening his eye's, he found himself in a small but rather nicely decorated room. Taking in his surroundings he realised he was in the living room. A big flat screen television was on the wall and it had a cabinet underneath housing different items. One of which he could identify as a stereo, the others he wasn't so familiar with.

Spotting some photographs on a wall, he headed for them. He recognised Isabella straight away. She was still as beautiful as ever and looked so much like his Constance. He smiled at the memory and glanced at another figure in the photograph. His eyes widened in surprise at how old his brother looked. If Richard stayed here any longer he would most certainly die. This only strengthened his resolve. He couldn't set off the call of the rose because he knew what would happen to his brother once he stepped back through to the Neutral Realm. Shuddering at that thought he busied himself with opening draws to find an address book or something that would lead him to this Sonya woman. None of the photographs contained her picture as they were all of Jordan and his family.

"Who the hell are you?" shrieked a woman's voice from behind him. He had been so engrossed in what he was looking for that he hadn't heard the front door being closed. He stood up slowly and faced the woman.

"I'm Vincent, Jordan's new roommate and you are?" he asked holding out his hand hoping he sounded believable.

"I'm Sonya Barton," she said shaking Vincent's hand. "Jordan didn't mention anything about getting a roommate."

"I have only been here a week, but he hasn't mentioned a Sonya. Do you know each other well?"

"We split up two weeks ago," Sonya replied shrugging.

The feeling of defeat smashed into Vincent's gut like a whirlwind. He wasn't going to be beaten. Suddenly he remembered the incident with his sister and Jordan's reaction. This woman could still be of some use to him.

"How could he let anything so beautiful go?" Vincent said raising her hand to his lips. He kept eye contact as he placed a tender kiss to the back of her hand. "Are you currently with anyone else?"

"Jordan's best friend Michael," she replied. Looking into his eyes she smiled sultrily at him. "But I could be persuaded if someone better came along." She fluttered her eye lashes at him and ran a finger over his shoulder.

Vincent fought the urge to roll his eyes. What was it with mortal women and the eye fluttering thing? He didn't have any love for his nephew, but he was pretty sure that Jordan could do better than this woman. Even now she was throwing him the 'take me to bed' signals. Vincent guessed the woman was probably what humans called a gold digger and a promiscuous one. Would she have the same reaction to him if he was in jeans and a T-shirt instead of the expensive Italian suit he currently wore.

"How long had you and Jordan been together?" Vincent asked, he was curious.

"Ten years. We got together when we were fifteen, in secondary school," Sonya said flatly.

"That's a long time to be with someone. Would you get back together with him given the chance?"

"Only if a certain blonde wasn't in the picture…. Anyway I don't want to talk about him, I would rather talk about you," she said smiling sweetly at him.

Vincent could feel her nails digging deeper into his skin and he really needed to get this show on the road. He hated the human realm with a passion and only ever ventured here to indulge in pleasures of the flesh. This woman was clearly going to be a willing participant. He would worry about the blonde she spoke of later, for now it was time to put his plan into action.

"Would you care to go out for a drink?" Vincent asked. He needed her to be intoxicated so she didn't notice when he flashed them to his boudoir in the Elven Realm.

"I thought you'd never ask," she said while grabbing his hand and leading him towards the front door.

Chapter Twenty-Six

Vincent led an intoxicated Sonya into his boudoir. The room was illuminated with the appropriate mood lighting. It didn't scream out gentle love making, nor did it scream out kinky stuff which he was partial too. Not tonight though, he hadn't done gentle since before his Constance died. Tonight was about the lust and passion and this woman Sonya had it in abundance. She was ripe for the taking and she had been trying to jump him all night. Getting her to the Elven Realm without her noticing hadn't been as hard as he thought.

Taking her lips with his own he placed his hands on the top of her hips and gently led her over to the four poster bed. The red velvet curtains were tied back revealing the red satin sheets on top of the bed which had been turned down, as if someone had been expecting him to have company tonight. He passed the white shaggy rug that sat in front of the fire place. A small fire in the grill added to the ambiance and warmth of the room. He made a mental note to make use of that at some point tonight. He had always been partial to shagging on a rug in front of a crackling fire.

Once they reached the bed, Vincent slid his hand up Sonya's back to her shoulders removing the straps. The dress glided down her slender body and ended up in a heap on the floor. His tie had already been removed and he couldn't help but admire the passion in her eyes. She fumbled trying to undo his shirt buttons in her haste to get him naked. When she finally managed to get them undone she quickly undid the button and zipper of his trousers, letting them fall to the floor at his ankles. He kicked them across the room to get them out of his way and started kissing across her jawline and down along her throat. He took in her delicious scent as he placed teasing little nips and sucks as he went. He made his way down to her voluptuous breasts which were cupped beautifully in her red lace bra.

Tracing his finger along the edge of the bra he enjoyed the rise and fall of her chest which matched his slow movements. He slipped a finger behind the decadent fabric and rubbed over her nipple. A small moan left her lips as her nipple hardened into a stiff peak. He moved to place his mouth where his finger was and sucked hard on the nipple through the fabric. He traced his fingers down her body to her centre, rubbing over the fabric of her underwear. He switched his attentions to her other breast as her breathy moans of ecstasy increased with every touch of his hands.

Her hand suddenly going to his man hood startled him. He grabbed it roughly and held it behind her back while he continued to devour her mouth with his. He lifted his hands to her shoulders and slowly pulled the straps of her bra down her arms. Reaching around her back he undid the clasp, letting the bra fall to join the dress on the floor. Kneeling in front of her he placed kisses across her abdomen and slowly removed her lace panties. Parting her thighs, he ran his tongue over her folds and tasted her. He could taste how ready she was for him. He kissed his way back up her body and felt her free his hair from its band, letting it flow freely over his shoulders.

He eased her body around so her back was facing him and fondled her breast. He kissed the back of her neck, enjoying the small moans she was making. Slowly he bent her over the bed so her hands rested on the silk sheets. He glided his hands down over her arse and ran his fingers through her folds rubbing his fingers over the hardened nub of her clit. He smirked with delight as he felt her body shudder under his manipulations. Her pussy was glistening with her juices and all he wanted to do was ram his cock into her and fuck her hard, so hard that she would be screaming for him to stop. He wanted to punish her, he wanted her to beg for mercy. He had to stop before he got carried away, so he kissed her shoulder instead, trying to calm his raging thoughts.

"You are so ready for me," he breathed into her ear. She whimpered in response so he grabbed his cock and nudged her entrance with it. Slowly he slid his thick cock into her. The gasp that escaped her lips clearly showed she hadn't been expecting it. He kissed slowly along the top of her shoulder blades and waited for her body to become accustomed to his size. Once she had settled he withdrew his cock slowly, loving the feel of being sheathed inside her wetness. He thrust back in hard needing to feel that pussy hugging his cock. Grabbing her hips, Vincent picked up the pace with every thrust. The only sounds in the room were the slapping of skin and their moans of ecstasy. He could feel her body tightening around him, gripping him like a vice as she climaxed screaming his name hysterically. He was so close to his own climax that her screams and the gripping of her pussy walls pulled the seed from his body. All his muscles tightened as he emptied himself inside of her, still feeling her shaking around him.

He withdrew from her warmth and picked her up placing her gently on the bed. She rested her head on the pillow panting from exhaustion before her breathing evened out and he knew she was asleep. Watching her he felt like a young Elf again, wanting a round two. He decided he would let her body rest a bit so he slipped on his silk robe and headed for the kitchen.

Waking sometime later Sonya turned her head to see Vincent lying on his back next to her. He had a satin sheet draped over the lower half of his body. One of his arms was resting on his chest and the other was bent at the elbow above his head. For her, he was breath-taking. Why hadn't she met him ten years ago? Her movements caught his attention and he turned his head to look at her. Smiling at her, he turned on his side and rested himself on his elbow. His black hair flowed down past his shoulders and pooled on the red satin pillow.

Butterflies fluttered in the pit of her stomach as she devoured him with her eyes. She reached over and ran a finger along his strong jaw and down his nicely toned body until she got to the top of the satin sheet. Her hand stopped and she bit her bottom lip, watching his expression. Slowly she moved the sheet down and revealed his impressive erection, making her mouth water and her pussy clench.

She sat up and didn't even notice the sheet fall from her body. She prowled towards him and placed her hands on his chest, pushing him on his back. She straddled his legs and placed her other hand around his now engorged penis. She leaned down and licked the tip and smiled as he let out a hiss between his teeth. Running her tongue slowly around the tip, she closed her lips around the head. She ran her tongue over the slit as she slowly moved her mouth down his long shaft. She opened her throat so she could accommodate all of him. Easing back up his length she sucked hard and rolled her tongue around the bulbous head before repeating the motion. The feel of his body tensing under her palm excited her. He bucked his hips which enticed her to move faster and deeper. She gently grabbed his balls and massaged them in her hand.

"Sonya," he growled.

It was a plea, so she stopped half way down his shaft and looked at him. His penis was still firmly in her mouth and she noticed the gleam in his eye as he cocked his finger at her. Releasing his throbbing manhood, she slowly crawled up his body stopping with her wet centre just above his cock. She kissed him as she rubbed her slick centre against his hardness.

"My god I want you," Vincent said between kisses.

"Not as much as I want you," Sonya replied as she slowly lowered herself onto him. Once completely seated, Vincent bucked his hips. She slowly rolled her hips and moved up and down his long shaft, picking up pace as she went. She didn't even stop when Vincent sat up and grabbed her hips, taking a nipple into his mouth. Sonya raised her arms and arched her back as he met her thrust for thrust.

She suddenly felt a jolt of pain run through her body. She looked down at Vincent, had he just bitten her? It sent a rush of pleasure through her and she rolled her hips harder and faster. She had an urge to tie him up but decided she would leave it for another day. An orgasm struck her hard and her muscles clamped around his shaft as ecstasy consumed her. She collapsed on Vincent feeling perfectly relaxed as he switched their positions. He pushed back into her again, feeling her body all over while sensually making love to her. She couldn't help biting back the smile at the change of pace. He thrusted himself deep inside her and tensed as he found his release. When he withdrew, she felt disappointed as he laid next to her. Slowly he placed his arm around her and dragged her closer to him. She snuggled into his warmth and couldn't help thinking there was nowhere she would rather be as she slowly closed her eyes and drifted off to sleep.

Chapter Twenty-Seven

Jordan opened his eyes slowly feeling a little sluggish, like he had been drinking all night. Not recognising where he was, he immediately went into a panic. Darting his eyes around he could make out the red velvet curtains tied to the bed posts and he could see notches carved into them. He really didn't want to know what they were for, even if he could take a wild guess and be right. He heard light breathing next to him and he slowly turned his head on the pillow. He jumped out of the bed, startled that someone was lying next to him.

"What the fuck," he screamed. He scrambled to his feet after tripping over the bed curtains in his haste to get out of the bed. The woman who had been sleeping peacefully next to him, sat bolt upright. Turning her head in his direction she used the red satin sheet to cover herself up.

"Sonya," he breathed.

"Jordan," she gasped pulling the sheet closer to her body. "What the hell are you doing in here?"

"Clearly not screwing you," he said. He was still fully dressed in his pyjama bottoms and singlet, which had a black scorch mark on it. "However someone has been," he said noticing the massive love bite on the top of her breast not covered by the sheet.

"That is none of your business," she said while manoeuvring the sheet and getting out bed.

"Your right it is none of my business. However, I would like to assume that it was Michael you slept with. What with him being the boyfriend and all." He couldn't help notice the way she looked around the room and bit her lower lip. "You didn't sleep with Michael, did you?"

"No I didn't," she said lifting her chin in a defensive manner.

"So who did you sleep with?" he asked curiously.

"Vincent."

"Vincent who?" he asked remembering the bloke from yesterday. He wondered if he was back home or still in the other realm. If he was in the other realm, how the hell did Sonya get here?

"Your new roommate."

"I don't have a roommate, new or otherwise"

"Yes you do, he told me so when I went to the flat yesterday. I was picking up some more of my stuff."

"So let me get this straight. You went to the flat to pick up some of your stuff and some strange bloke was there. He claimed to be my new roommate and at some point during the night you fucked him," Jordan said as he paced the room. "Knowing you like I do probably two maybe three times in one night, how am I doing so far?"

"It was four times and he was better than you and Michael put together." Her voice was laced with barely contained anger. She couldn't believe how close he had been to the truth or how it made her sound. She knew it was childish to attempt to belittle his ability in the bedroom, but she just couldn't help herself.

"Have you actually split with Michael?" Jordan had to find out, and was curious as hell about it as well.

"When you say split…?"

"Yes or no, it's a simple question." Jordan had stopped his pacing to glare at her.

"No I haven't."

"So you have cheated on him and before that you cheated on me with him. Tell me Sonya, the ten years that we were together did you cheat on me for the whole time or was it just the last few weeks with Michael?"

"Umm…"

"You have got to be fucking kidding me."

"It wasn't the whole time," she said defensively.

"How many years have you been cheating me?" He couldn't believe it. It felt like he had been punched in the gut.

"About four," she said shrugging.

"Four." Jordan was totally gobsmacked and was struggling with his emotions. Hurt, anger and betrayal blindsided him all at once. This really was a conversation they should have had weeks ago, had he not been in shock from seeing her and Michael going at it like rabbits.

"So when did the cheating start?"

"After the school ball."

"What school ball?"

"Jessica's."

"Didn't we split up for like two weeks around that time?" Jordan remembered the night, He went to comfort an upset Charlotte and calm a very pissed off Jessica. He couldn't see what her problem was with that.

"It was because of that night we split up, you prick," Sonya practically yelled.

"How was it?" Jordan yelled back.

"Well, if you hadn't dropped everything to be a knight in shining armour to that annoying Charlotte."

"You leave her the fuck out of this." Jordan hadn't even realised he had been pointing his finger in her face, until she slapped his had away.

"No I won't," she said collecting the end of the sheet in her arms. She took a step closer to him. "It was because of her, I started cheating on you. It was only a matter of time before you cheated on me with her."

"You are so full of shit. Charlotte is my sister's best friend and is like a sister to me. There is no way I would have fucked her."

"Your absolutely right, my apologies," she said bowing to him.

"About what? You, sarcastic bitch."

"You wouldn't have fucked her." Sonya slowly walked around Jordan as she continued, "You my darling, would have made sweet passionate love to her, making her feel like she was the only woman in the world."

"Bollocks."

"And here we have the classic end of an argument comment." Sonya stopped and faced him as she continued. "Do you have any idea what it felt like having to compete with her?"

"You are full of shit. If you recall, Jessica and Charlotte are inseparable. When I go to see my sister, she just happens to be there. You are jealous of the closeness I have with my sisters, always have been."

"I wouldn't be if that was the case…my god Jordan how can you be so blind," she screeched.

"Blind to what, you cheating on me for four years. Yes, I was blind to that. Now you are making up stuff that is totally crap to try and account for your actions." Jordan started stalking towards Sonya making her retreat. "You are nothing but an unfaithful bitch."

"You're being a bit polite there, aren't you?" Vincent said as Jordan and Sonya spun their heads in his direction. Clearly they hadn't heard him enter the room. "Tell her the truth, she is nothing but a worthless whore."

The look of horror on Sonya's face made Vincent smirk but Jordan's displayed some anger. Vincent would soon find out if his nephew was the chivalrous type, as he suspected.

"You bastard," Sonya shrieked. The sound made both Jordan and Vincent wince.

"I'm sorry was gold digger a better description? I mean seriously, would you have been so willing to sleep with a man you know nothing about if you didn't think he was loaded." It only occurred to Vincent then that she hadn't noticed that his features had gone back to his Elven form.

"This is the man you thought was my flatmate," Jordan asked pointing at Vincent. He remembered him from yesterday with Trixie. "Do you even know where the hell you are?"

"Yes I did and no I don't know where I am, still in London I hope."

"You're in another realm."

"Now who's full of shit." Sonya glanced at Jordan before turning to Vincent. "You're not his flatmate are you?"

"No my dear I am not, never have been. I got a pretty good night out of it though. Who would have thought you would be so easy?"

"How dare you."

"How dare I, for what stating the truth. You met a man who claims to be your ex's flatmate and then you're screwing him less than four hours later. Not to mention being in a relationship with someone else. You are nothing but a worthless whore, like I said before."

Vincent didn't even have time to react as Sonya came flying at him slapping him across the face and screeching at him in the process. On impulse he raised his arm and back handed her face, sending her body flying across the room. She hit the wall and slumped to the ground in a heap.

Looking at Sonya on the ground, he was yet again taken off guard. He was shocked when he heard a war cry pierce the room and was tackled to the ground by Jordan. It took a few punches from Jordan before Vincent was able to get a handle on what was happening. His nephew had a strong punch and Vincent knew if he didn't get this situation under control, he would be knocked out cold.

Blocking the next punch, he gave Jordan one of his own and wrestled him over onto his back before giving him another punch. He grabbed Jordan by the front of his singlet and dragged him up from the floor. He caught a glimpse of Lampros and his other guards in the door way so he used his power behind his next punch and sent Jordan flying into the bed post and knocking him out cold.

Rubbing the back of his hand over his lip, he winced at the pain. It had been a while since he had a split lip.

"Take him to the dungeon," he told his guards. They seemed to look at Lampros and only moved after his signal. Vincent assumed he had ordered them not to interfere.

"What of her?" One of his guards asked while they were leading Jordan out of the room.

Vincent looked at a now stirring Sonya. He couldn't believe he wanted her again. What the hell was wrong with him. "Leave her to me," he said sternly as the younger Elves left the room. A very smug looking Lampros stayed behind.

"What are you looking so smug for?" Vincent asked while smoothing out his clothes.

"Nothing, just your fighting style."

"What about my fighting style?"

"Rusty aren't you," Lampros said grinning widely.

"I'll show you rusty," Vincent said raising his fist to carry through with his threat.

"Any time mate, you know I can best you…However," he said pointing over to a now awake Sonya. "You might want to deal with your latest trollop."

"Wanker," Sonya shouted as she stood up.

"On occasion," Lampros called back as he left the room, laughing.

Vincent looked over at Sonya. The glare she fired at him was enough to make any man wary. He really hadn't meant to smack her as hard as he did. He also knew that he wasn't quite ready for her to go yet either. It would seem that his body wasn't finished with the woman. He had some serious grovelling to do and he was at least seventy years out of practice.

Chapter Twenty-Eight

After chaining Jordan up in the middle of the dungeon, Vincent stepped back to look at his nephew. He was still unconscious and was just hanging there. His arms were above his head and his chin was resting on his chest. Vincent could feel Jordan's power flowing into him but it wasn't enough. Vincent was again using his power to keep Jordan unconscious sensing Trixie in the Elven realm. He needed to come up with a way to throw her off Jordan's scent.

Walking towards the small arched window in the dungeon, he stopped in front of a small metal basin. Pulling a knife from the confines of his cloak he made a small slit across his palm. He watched the red liquid flow into the bowl and placed a finger into the liquid and started swirling it around. "Ruby, I summon thy." A slight breeze blew across the room and Vincent turned around to see a beautiful woman. Her long red velvet dress was moulded to her form.

"What the hell are you doing summoning me, I was busy with a rather dishy pixie," she said glaring at Vincent.

Vincent knelt down in front of the woman and grabbed her hand, placing a kiss on her knuckles. He looked up at her, "I thought I was the only object of your desire?"

"Please, if I was going to be faithful to someone what makes you think it would be you?" she asked pulling her hand out of Vincent's. "Now what do you want?" She took note of her surroundings and continued. "I take it this isn't a booty call unless you're into whips and chains…. Oh that's right, you are. Not normally in the dungeon though, is this a new phase?"

"I need your help in shielding someone," Vincent answered getting straight to the point.

"Shielding who?" Ruby asked.

"Does it matter?" Vincent asked not really wanting to tell her.

"It does if you want my help, now who is it?" Ruby replied as she put her hands on her hips and glared at him.

"My nephew," Vincent said and motioned to where he had Jordan chained up.

Ruby turned her head and her heart sank. It was the young man she had spent a great night with two days ago and he was chained up. She wished there was something she could do to help him for Richard's sake, but there wasn't. She knew he would be pissed when he found out. She also knew that it wouldn't help the young man at all to give away the fact that she knew him, so she pretended she didn't.

"Well isn't he handsome." She looked at Vincent as she slowly walked towards Jordan. "How about you leave the room and I wake this gorgeous young man up and have some fun." She stopped suddenly when Vincent stood between her and his nephew. She pinched his cheeks like he was a five-year-old. "Is the evil elf jealous of his nephew."

Vincent just glared at her. "Can you shield him or not?"

"Depends," Ruby replied shrugging.

"On what," Vincent said narrowing his eyes at her while folding his arms over his chest.

"On whom he is to be shielded from and what the shielding will entail."

"I need him hidden," Vincent answered not changing his stance as he looked at her.

"Hidden from whom?" Ruby asked raising an eyebrow at him.

"Trixie…. No everyone but me, nobody can see him or sense him. Can you do that?"

"Yes that's easy, however the enchantment is not full proof."

"Meaning?" he asked with slight frustration in his voice.

"Is Richard still in the Human Realm?" she asked Vincent raising an eyebrow at him again.

"Yes," Vincent answered. He wondered why she asked about his brother's whereabouts'.

"Good," she said taking a step closer to Jordan. She conjured a bowl out of thin air and using the same knife Vincent had used to summon her, she made a long slit down Jordan's arm. She caught the droplets of blood in the bowl and she passed Vincent the knife. "You know the deal."

Taking the knife, Vincent slit his own arm adding his blood to the bowl. Once done he stood back from Ruby as a gust of wind came from nowhere, surrounding her. Raising the bowl above her head she began to chant. Vincent couldn't make out what she was saying all he could do was watch as the wind thrashed her long black hair all over the place. Her eyes took on an unhealthy glow. Just as quick as the wind had started, it stopped.

"It's done," Ruby said as she turned to look at him.

"That's it?" Vincent said.

"What did you expect…. Fireworks?" she said sarcastically.

"So I'm the only one who can see him and sense him"

Ruby looked at Vincent knowing exactly what he was doing with his nephew. She also knew that she couldn't hide him from Richard. Spell or no spell he would still be able to see and sense his son where nobody else could, except for maybe his soul mate.

"Yes, you are the only one." Ruby replied rolling her eyes at him.

"Good," he said rubbing his hands with glee.

Ruby caught the smug look on Vincent's face. She hoped Jordan didn't wake up while someone was in the room with Vincent. He hadn't asked for Jordan not to be heard. With a smug smile of her own, she addressed Vincent in a formal manner.

"The spell will be broken when the king returns."

With a click of her fingers she was gone.

Chapter Twenty-Nine

Jordan slowly started regaining consciousness and couldn't understand why he was feeling groggy. He felt like he had been out drinking all night. Not yet opening his eyes he tried to get his mind around why he felt the way he did. He ached all over and felt exhausted. Had he gone out drinking and ended up being up all night? He just couldn't remember. He came to the realisation that he was, in fact, up right. His arms were above his head so he focused on that.

He could feel cold metal around his wrists, digging into his flesh. He tried to open his eyes and lift his head but found he was unable to. He noticed he wasn't even on his feet and he didn't have the energy to attempt to stand. He was just hanging limp like a rag doll.

What the hell was wrong with him and where the hell was he. He tried to control the panic he felt rising in his chest. He felt another heavy weight on his neck and chest. Using all his effort he slowly managed to open one of his eyes. His chin was resting on his chest and he noticed what looked like a gem set in a thick gold chain. If you could even call it a chain. It looked more like someone had taken one of the old mirrors from his grandparents' house and turned it into a necklace, adding various gems around the edge. It was so heavy, which had to be why he felt so exhausted. Why it was around his neck, he couldn't even begin to comprehend.

He realised that the chain around his neck was the same chain that Vincent had tried to give him a few days ago. He had been adamant that he was to wear it but why? He couldn't help but wonder, especially since he seemed to be wearing it now.

He couldn't help wonder if the necklace had something to do with why he was feeling so low on his energy. He figured he had to try and get the thing off and with luck, nobody would hear the clunk on the floor once he managed it.

"I can't hang around here all day," he said to himself trying to lighten the mood he was in. Not that he knew how he would get out of the situation, but at least having a plan was better than nothing. "Time to get this thing off me."

Since Jordan was hanging, he tried moving his legs to see if he was actually off the ground. Feeling the ground beneath his ankles, he slowly moved his legs. He realised he could stand on his own merit. Straightening his legs, he could instantly feel the release of pressure from his shoulders as his arms lowered a fraction. Gritting his teeth through that pain he tried to roll his shoulders as best he could, feeling a little bit better now that he was on his feet and not hanging like a lump.

Moving his head back to see how he was chained, he noticed the shackles were connected to smaller chains that connected by a ring to a larger one. He followed the trail of chains that ended at the wall by the door. It looked like some old medieval system with a metal handle that looked like a chain. It wound around the handle and was turned and locked in place by another lever.

Shaking his wrists slightly so the shackles moved a little further down his arm he grasped the two smaller chains, tugging slightly to see if he could somehow unhinge it but it didn't move. Disappointment seeped into his gut. Clearly he couldn't shake the chain free. He wasn't going to be beaten though, he would get the necklace off one way or another. He just hoped it wouldn't be the last thing he did.

Getting a tighter grip on the smaller chains, he used what upper body strength he could to lift himself. Three inches later he dropped back down, that clearly wasn't going to work. If only he could climb up the main chain. Standing on his tip toes, he bypassed the smaller chains and managed to reach the thicker chain. Getting a tighter grip and gritting his teeth, he started climbing, legs out straight in front of him. Finally, the two years of army cadets his mother sent him to were paying off.

Getting half way up the chain, he tried to flip himself over so his legs could grab the chain above his head and the necklace would just fall off. After two attempts and plummeting back to the ground, he was surprised he hadn't dislocated his shoulders. The amount of pain he was in, he probably had for all he knew. It suddenly dawned on him, that he didn't need to flip himself at all.

Having renewed strength, he grabbed the chain and climbed again, not going as high this time. He stopped where he could actually reach his hands, the chain making a loop at the end. Placing his knee in the loop, he gripped the chain a little tighter, resting his shoulder on it to give him some stability. He let go of the chain with his other hand and as quick as he could, removed the chain from around his neck.

The necklace dropped to the ground and he enjoyed the thud it made. He slowly unhooked himself and lowered himself to the ground.

Jordan could feel his strength returning but it was a little too late. Yet again darkness blurred his vision as he slipped into unconsciousness.

Chapter Thirty

Trixie woke up to water being splashed on her face. When she opened her eyes she realised she was leaning up against a tree.

"Fall asleep did you?" Lampros asked her.

"Well obviously," she replied. She stood and brushed the dead leaves from her clothes. "What the hell did you do that for?"

"What the water?"

"No, the kiss to awaken sleeping beauty…. yes, the bloody water," she said as she glared at him.

"I thought I saw dirt on your face."

"You are a tosser," she said while pointing her finger in his face. She turned and stormed off towards the castle. "Is my bloody brother back yet?" she snapped.

"Yes and he sent me to come and get you," he said. He rushed to catch up, she really could move fast when she was angry.

"I'll bet he did," she muttered. Trixie had made it half way down the stone path leading up to the castle gates when she stopped so suddenly that Lampros collided with her. The force sent them both falling to the ground, hard. He hadn't realised how close he was to catching up with her.

"Shit," Lampros said in a panic. He got back up quickly and started checking her over.

"Get off me," she said slowly sitting up. She held the side of her head which hit the stone path. She noticed the other side of the path which had a build-up of unmown lawn and wondered why they hadn't fallen in that direction. Her head definitely wouldn't be hurting as much as it did now. The throbbing started to give her a headache. She could clearly see her brother in the castle laughing his head off, yeah he'd definitely seen their little tumble. 'Bastard', she thought as she got to her feet.

"Why the hell did you stop so suddenly," Lampros asked raising a hand to the bump now forming on Trixie's head. He was more concerned for her pain than his own.

"I will let you know once this throbbing stops and I can think straight," she said as she started once again making her way to the castle, a little slower this time however.

Once they reached the castle gates, they didn't have time to knock before Vincent was standing before them grinning like an idiot. Trixie wanted to smack the grin of his face.

"Trixie darling how wonderful to see you," Vincent said taking a step closer and giving her a small hug before placing a kiss on each of her cheeks.

"I'm sure it is," she replied coldly. The feeling of unease she had before her tumble with Lampros returned. That's why she had stopped, feeling something was off. The way Vincent was now acting only confirmed it. Not to mention the fact that she could no longer sense her nephew.

"Come little sister I have a meal prepared," he said putting his arms around her shoulders and leading her through the large castle doors. Even Lampros had a look of confusion on his face.

"I'm not hungry," Trixie said to her brother. Her stomach suddenly rumbling made a liar out of her. She didn't even realise she hadn't eaten since breakfast with Jordan, the day before. "Where is our nephew?" she asked as they entered a large dining room. A long table sat in the middle of the room and various food dishes were visible from the door.

Vincent led Trixie to the head of the table and placed her on his left side, as Lampros seated himself opposite Trixie. Vincent took his place at the head of the table deliberately as it was higher than the other seats along the table. He wanted to show who their superior was, like anyone needed reminding.

"Vincent, where's our nephew?" she asked again. She grabbed a slice of toast and jam. It hadn't escaped her notice that he hadn't answered her question.

"He's not here," Vincent replied as he put a piece of buttery croissant into his mouth. Avoiding her gaze, he ripped off another part of his croissant and popped it into his mouth.

"Well where the hell is he?" she snapped.

"I sent him home."

"You sent him home?" Trixie repeated, not convinced. She knew that Jordan was basically stuck here. Did Vincent think she was an idiot or didn't know how this worked? She played along realising he had to be here somewhere. Even if she couldn't sense him. "So why did you take him?" she asked picking up her coffee cup bringing it to her lips.

"Tracey, I am not the evil uncle you seem to be making me out to be." Trixie almost chocked on her coffee with that comment. "I told you I wanted to spend some time with my nephew, and I did."

"And his ex," Lampros muttered under his breath, as he reached for the fruit bowl. Vincent glared at him, hearing what he said.

"What?" Trixie asked not quite catching the murmur.

"Nothing…. Fruit?" Lampros asked, putting the bowl under her nose.

"No thank you," she said pushing the bowl away. She steered the conversation back to Jordan. "So when did you send him home and how?"

"For fuck sake, I sent him home through the bloody mirror about an hour ago…. I suppose you want to see around the castle to prove he is not here."

"Yes actually, I would," she said while giving her brother a smart arse smile. What kind of an idiot did he take her for?

"Fine let's go," he said while standing up.

"But we haven't finished eating," Trixie said looking up at her brother.

"Tough, you wanted to see around the damn castle, so you're going to see around the damn castle.... now move it," he said storming off towards the doors, his cloak bellowing behind him.

Trixie followed Vincent to every room in the castle. Her feet were killing her, but she didn't let on. She knew he was doing it deliberately. Reaching one of the main corridors, he stopped and turned to look at her.

"Are you happy now?"

"No."

"NO," he bellowed at her. Lampros placed himself between the arguing siblings.

"No, you missed the dungeon."

"The dungeon?" he said raising his eyebrows at her. She pinned him with a look. "Fine," he said with a huff and headed towards the dungeon. He had to see if the spell worked and what better person to test it on.

Vincent had shown her all the rooms in the dungeon but one. He opened the door to the last cell in the dungeon and went in first. Trixie refused to go in first. Did she think he would trap her in one of the rooms? Chance would have been a fine thing but with Lampros so close behind them, it wasn't going to happen. Holding the door wide open he entered and once inside he motioned with his other hand for her to enter the room. She entered, followed closely by Lampros who stopped in the door way.

"See are you happy now? Jordan is nowhere in the castle." Vincent looked over the room and he could clearly see Jordan, right where he left him.

"I guess so," Trixie said flatly, looking around the cell. Something caught her eye.

"Vincent?"

"Yes?"

"Isn't that the cursed necklace?" she asked.

"What.... Where?"

"Over there," she said pointing at the necklace before making her way over to it and picking it up.

"I must have dropped it," Vincent said as he snatched the thing from his sister's hand.

"You dropped it in the dungeon?" she asked raising her eyebrows.

"Yes."

"Why is it not in the velvet box? You rarely take it out of that."

"Because I broke the bloody box when I threw it against the wall. I put the necklace in my pocket…. why the hell am I explaining myself to you?"

"I don't know, maybe you're a lying son of a bitch and your trying to convince me otherwise," she said while smiling at her brother, knowing it would really piss him off.

"Lampros."

"Yeah," he said standing straight.

"Would you be so kind as to escort my sister back to the main elf castle or her own one in the spring valley…or better yet just dump her in the neutral realm."

"What…that's it?" Trixie asked flabbergasted.

"Yes little sister, you have worn out your welcome for the day. Good bye," he said while turning his back on her. She stormed to the door of the dungeon and was gone.

Chapter Thirty-One

Vincent watched from the window of the dungeon as Trixie and Lampros walked down the path towards the forest. If he didn't know better, he would swear that they were having an argument. No doubt started by his sister. He waited until they were out of sight before turning to his nephew. The spell had clearly worked, however the necklace being on the floor was a little inconvenient. How had his nephew gotten the necklace off and when?

He could feel that Jordan's strength had returned, so he guessed the necklace had been off for a while. When was the last time he had been fed? Not wanting to be a complete bastard he left to retrieve a meal for his nephew.

Returning with the two metal trays, he set them on the floor. He picked a spot on the floor and parked his bum. Waving his hand in the direction of the chain wheel, he slowly lowered his nephew to the ground. He sent a small bolt of lightning at his nephew to wake him up. Vincent could see the pain on his nephew's face as he lowered his arms. He had been hanging there for a while now.

"Eat," Vincent said while sliding the tray towards his nephew. Jordan just raised an eyebrow at him. "You can pick one if it will make you feel better, neither have been tampered with."

"Thanks," Jordan said in a garbled voice. His throat was as dry as sandpaper. Slowly reaching over he grabbed the edge of the tray closest to Vincent and slid it over. He hadn't realised how hungry he was until the smell of food caught his nose. Looking at the cafeteria style tray of food he took in what he had been served. An apple, a coffee, water, a sandwich of some kind and slop. He picked up the fork but let it fall back onto the tray.

"It's stew, it does taste better than it looks." Vincent informed him as he took a mouthful of it.

Jordan ate in silence, keeping a wary eye on the elf sitting before him. Once the tray had been cleared of every last morsel including the slop which was rather delicious, Jordan focused his attention on the elf.

"Vincent, wasn't it?" he enquired.

"That's correct."

"Why am I chained up in a dungeon?" Jordan felt like he was on the set of a medieval film.

"You struck a prince of the realm, that is usually punishable by death."

"You struck a woman, I was sure as hell not going to stand there and do nothing."

"Would you have done that for any woman or was it that particular one?"

"I would have done it for any female. I wouldn't want to be sent to my death because of Sonya.... where is she?" he said, only just noticing he was alone in the dungeon.

"She is safe and has been well taken care of."

"I bet she has," he said sarcastically. "So what makes me so special, not to be put to death?"

"The king would kill me, which is why I have caused you no harm. The last thing I want is to face my brothers' wrath.... Again." Vincent replied. "And I wouldn't like my chances against your mother either," he said while placing his tray on the floor.

"My mother?" Jordan said raising his eyebrows.

"Yes, what is that expression 'hell hath no fury than a woman scorned.' They are even worse when their off spring are in danger. Your mother is a very powerful woman. She probably hasn't even got a clue about half the stuff she is actually capable of."

"What are you talking about? You don't even know my mother."

"Isabella was once a very good friend of mine," Vincent said as he stood up and walked over to the chain wheel. He slowly raised his nephew off the ground and Jordan had no choice but to stand as the chain went up.

"So what happened then?" It didn't escape his notice that Vincent hadn't sent the chains up over his head like before. He currently had plenty of movability, as his hands hung down in front of his groin.

"I tried to seduce her, knowing she was not mine to have. The king kind of lost it with me. Your father does have a very vicious temper on the odd occasion he loses it."

"It sounded like you were implying that my father is a king of some sort?"

"Who's implying," Vincent said smiling. He felt for the necklace in his pocket. With its weight, he was surprised he had forgotten it was in there. "Your father is King of the Elven Realm."

"And my Mother?" Jordan asked, thinking the man was full of crap.

"Is of Witch and Fae decent." Vincent gave his nephew a bland look, either he was taking this news well or didn't believe a word of it.

"So let me get this straight, my mother is a witch slash Fae and my father is what, King of the Elves. Have I got that clear?"

"Yes."

"And they both have powers of some kind?" It was more a question than a statement of fact.

"Yes." Vincent was starting to get frustrated with his nephew and his questions, "As I have said, your mother wouldn't have a clue about her full potential. I wouldn't want to go up against her powers, she would be very unpredictable. Your father on the other hand, I know what he can do. I can't beat him in a powers battle, except maybe by sheer luck. He will always be stronger than me apparently. However, I would like to prove that theory wrong."

"How do you plan do that then?"

"By accumulating more powers of course, preferably from someone of equal power to myself." Vincent said as he gave his nephew a sly smile.

Jordan didn't like the look he was getting which made his gut tighten with dread. He couldn't help recall the story his nan had told him. 'The young prince being taken by his evil uncle for his powers.' The elf standing in front of him would be his uncle, he may not have said it straight out but had suggested it. Did that mean he had powers as well? He sure as hell didn't feel any different.

"I gather you already have an idea of whose powers you plan to take," Jordan asked raising an eyebrow at the elf.

"Yes I do." Vincent smiled as he pulled the necklace from his pocket and took a step towards his nephew.

"You think I have powers?" Jordan asked incredulously.

"Oh but you do, an abundance of them. They feel like they match my own. Although with your powers so out of control it is a little hard to tell."

"And your what? Just going to take the powers. The powers that I don't have by the way."

"Yes."

"What no offer to turn me to the dark side? Or train me to use my powers for your own benefit? You're just going to take them, how?"

"With this," he said as he held up the necklace. "As I have said before I don't mean you any harm. This necklace will slowly transfer your powers to me."

"And what will happen to me?

"You will just pass out after most of your powers have been transferred."

"So I won't die then?"

"No. If I was to force the power transfer, then you would be in excruciating pain and most likely die. I would be very surprised if you didn't, everybody else has."

"How would you force the power transfer?" Jordan was curious.

"By using an electrical force, with the sole purpose to take the powers."

"Kind of like the Sith powers."

"Yes, just like the Sith powers," he said rolling his eyes. "You are as bad as your bloody Aunt Trixie."

"So do all Elves hold this power?" Jordan asked before catching what he just said. "Trixie is my Aunt?"

"Yes all Elves hold that power. Even your father who has never used the ability and yes, Trixie is your Aunt and she loves those damn films." He took a step towards Jordan and raised his arm, the necklace in his hand.

"What the hell are you doing?" Jordan asked taking a step back. He knew he couldn't get too far away being in chains, but he could use them to his advantage if he had too.

"I'm going to put this necklace on you, you will feel the effects straight away as it drains your powers."

"You come near me and I will wrap this chain around your fuck-ing neck."

Vincent paused in his steps and watched his nephew closely. He couldn't tell if the man was being serious or just bluffing. Erring on the side of caution, Vincent waved his hand towards the main chain lever and watched as the chains rose. "Why are you being so difficult, I said I meant you no harm." Vincent stepped closer to Jordan cautiously as he knew his nephew could still use his legs.

"You are a lying son of a bitch."

"Am I?"

"Yes, you say you mean me no harm but clearly this will not be good for me in the long run. You are power hungry, syphoning my powers in secret so you don't piss off my dad. You are clearly shit scared of him because you are weak. Then what? Once you have my powers are you going to try to take out my father? Which would then what… Make me the new king and in my weakened state, you would then be able to dispose of me. Have I missed anything in your grand plan?"

"No, that about some's it up." Vincent replied shrugging.

"So why not just force the powers from me?"

"Because you little insect, that would set off the call of the rose. This would bring your father back and he wouldn't be the old man he is now. I grow impatient with waiting for him to die in the human realm. By the time that happened, I would have you to deal with. You would be king and you would know how to use your powers. Not only that but you would be more powerful. I'm taking this chance I have and using it to my advantage."

"So, you are scared." Jordan said with a gleam in his eye. He was goading the elf and he knew it. He didn't want to be in agony but he had to believe that there was some truth to his Grandmothers story's. If not, he would be dead any way. Either before his father died or after, if Vincent's plan succeeded. What did he have to lose at this point?

"I am not."

"Prove it, or are you too much of a coward? What? You scared your big brother will kick your fucking arse?"

"I am no coward," Vincent said between clenched teeth. He tried to keep his anger in check but found himself getting up in his nephew's face.

Jordan smiled, knowing he was hitting the right nerves.

"You are all mouth and no action. You can't do half the stuff you claim to be able to do. You're a coward and you are weak. Stealing someone else's powers to make you feel stronger." Vincent walked a few feet away from Jordan trying to contain his rage. "You are weak Vincent, weak. I will take great pleasure in watching my father kick your sorry arse."

"You are pushing your luck boy," Vincent said glaring at his nephew. Never had someone shown Vincent such disrespect.

"And your bluffing, because you can't do shit." An agonising pain shot through Jordan's body without warning. He didn't even realise the screams of pain he was hearing were coming from him. Jordan cursed himself, what had he been thinking in provoking the man?

Vincent was getting a rush from the power drain and it was over-whelming. No longer could he hear Jordan's screams of agony. He used both hands to get the power faster. This increased the pain Jordan was feeling. He was so drunk on power that he didn't even notice when Jordan stopped screaming. A shockwave of power suddenly flew out of Jordan hitting him in the chest and sending him flying across the cell. He hit the stone wall with a crack which knocked him out cold.

Chapter Thirty-Two

Lampros quickly returned to the castle. He knew that something bad had happened. The Call of the Rose was being sent off across the realms. It was calling back all elves, no matter where they were. A strange throbbing sensation pulsed throughout his body. He instinctively knew what it was and knew what it meant.

Reaching the castle gates, he observed the younger elves looking confused. It never occurred to him that they had never been told about the call. It had been a long time since it was last activated, so long that it hadn't even happened in his life-time.

"General Lampros, what's happening?" A frightened young guard asked while standing to attention.

"The Call of the Rose has been set off."

"What does that mean, Sir?" another guard asked.

"That means, not only is a member of the royal family in life threatening danger, but the king will be returning within the day."

"But the king is in the castle?" The young elves both said in confusion.

"Vincent is not the god damn king," Lampros murmured. He clenched his fists at his side and walked through the gates. If the younger elves heard him say that, they would no doubt arrest him for treason. Given the situation, it wouldn't be a bad thing.

He headed down the main corridor, its narrow passageway was dimly lit with torches lining the walls. He was headed straight to the dungeon, the last place he had seen Vincent. He knew the call wasn't for Trixie because he had just left her. If the call was Richard in danger it would have been a lot stronger and he would have been flashed straight to the king. He doubted it was for Vincent, but thought he had better check any way. His gut was telling him it was Jordan in danger and Vincent was the cause. He hoped Vincent wasn't that stupid. If it was Jordan then where was he, or even more importantly how was he being hidden?

He spotted an unconscious Vincent against the wall when he reached the cell door. Dread seeped into the pit of his stomach. He bolted over to him and crouched down beside him.

"Vincent," he said, shaking him by the shoulders.

"What?" A groggy sounding Vincent answered.

"What the hell happened?"

Vincent slowly opened his eyes and sat up. He reached behind his head and felt a rather large lump. "Shit," Vincent said as he stood up. He went to the centre of the room and used his powers to lower the chain.

Lampros stood there bewildered. Vincent looked like he was checking someone over but, he couldn't see anyone.

"That's interesting," said Vincent before he stood and left the room.

Lampros watched Vincent leave and looked over to the area where Vincent had been standing once again. The shackles looked like someone was in them. You would have to be looking pretty closely to even notice.

"I wonder," he said making his way over to the shackles. His foot hit something he couldn't see or sense. Crouching down he felt around where his foot was and he could definitely feel there was someone there. "Fucking bastard," he whispered. He knew exactly what his best friend had done.

Closing his eyes, he felt as gently as he could to see if there were any signs of life in the still body. He didn't expect there to be any. He knew what happened when Vincent used the electric lightning. He drained a person's powers and killed them in the process. A lesser being would just be turned to dust after the process was complete.

"Well I'll be damned," he breathed. Lampros could feel the rise and fall of the man's chest. It was very light but he could feel it. Jordan should have been dead. Lampros smiled with relief. The realm must have stepped in somehow to protect the future king.

With that thought in mind Lampros left the dungeon and headed towards the main Elf castle.

Chapter Thirty-Three

Isabella sat in her favourite chair by the window in the lounge-room. She was happily working on her embroidery as the sun shone through her white net curtains. She wondered how Jordan was getting on and if he'd found out that her parents were still alive and kicking yet. Suddenly Isabella had a feeling of dread and she couldn't quite put her finger on it. She was suddenly thrown backwards in her chair by an invisible force like a bolt of lightning going right through her. The mirror above the fire place was glowing and looked like it was throbbing. The same throbbing now pulsing through her own body. She stood up and headed straight for it.

"RICHARD," Isabella yelled in a panic.

Slowly Richard walked into the living room and found his wife standing by the fire place looking towards the large mirror. You could see the fear on her beautiful face. Isabella looked up into his usually blue eyes which were now glowing silver.

"Do you feel that?" she asked, already knowing the answer.

Richard nodded. "The Call of the Rose," he answered with no emotion.

"You know what that means?" Isabella said. She walked to stand in front of her husband, placing her palms flat on his chest.

"I've got to go back." Looking down at his wife he said, "You know what will happen when I do."

"I do," she breathed. She knew full well that the call was being sent out and all of the warriors ages would be reset. If they don't return to the realm within twelve hours, they will be automatically flashed back.

"And you still want me to go?" he asked even though he actually didn't have a choice. Being King he was needed more than most and he knew the call could only mean one thing.

Isabella looked up into her husband's eyes, eyes she had not seen in many years and answered. "I don't want you to go and I sure as hell don't want to say you got vain about your looks and went to America for cosmetic surgery. Even though the comments would be interesting when you got back," she said trying to lighten the mood. "But you have too…. Our son is in danger"

"How do you know it's our son who is in danger?"

"Because if it was Trixie or Vincent, I wouldn't be getting the call…. I can't go through at the moment anyway. The realm is only calling for the full bloods."

"Sweetheart, the realm is summoning back elves only at the moment. You my love are not an elf," he said as he placed a kiss on her forehead.

"Yeah well it should include the mother of the next king."

"And it will, when the time is right. If it makes you feel any better, you will be sent for, before anyone else."

"Just go get ready and stop trying to make me feel better," Isabella said shaking her head at her husband.

It wasn't long before Isabella was standing at the front door waving. Richard was pulling out of the drive way of their London home. It was taking her all her effort not to fall to pieces worrying about her son. She smiled, holding back tears and blew her husband a kiss as he drove off.

Feeling a vibration in her pocket, she reached inside and grabbed her phone.

"Hello," she said not seeing who the caller was.

"Mum, thank god I got hold of you," said Jessica in a panic.

"What is it sweetheart?" Isabella asked trying to keep calm. The last thing she needed was Jessica in a frenzy considering whatever was happening to Jordan.

"You have to come over, it's Charlotte," Jessica screeched.

"What about Charlotte, is she okay?" Damn it. Now Isabella was really starting to worry.

"God, I don't know. She just started screaming in agony and collapsed on the bathroom floor."

"Why didn't you call the doctor?"

"I thought of you first because you used to be a nurse."

That was years ago Isabella thought as she took a deep breath, trying to calm herself. It wouldn't do anyone any good if she was to fall apart now. There would be time for that later.

"I will be right there," she said while grabbing her car keys from the hook. She took her coat off the rack and left the house, closing the door behind her.

Chapter Thirty-Four

Jordan stood in the hall way of his sister's house and shook his head in confusion. How did he get here? Last thing he recalled was Vincent using what he could only describe as electricity bolts on him and the excruciating pain it had caused. He had been warned about them. Looking around he noticed he wasn't even in the clothes he had on earlier. He now wore his favourite faded blue jeans, a tight white t-shirt and leather jacket with his nightclub shoes on. The sound of his sister's voice directed his attention towards the bathroom.

When he reached the bathroom door, he saw his sister's best friend Charlotte hunched over in pain. A concerned Jessica was crouching down next to her friend. Not wanting to startle them, he leaned up against the door frame and folded his arms watching them. He couldn't shake the concern he was feeling for Charlotte. He had known her since she was five and looked out for her like he did his sisters, maybe even more so, if he was completely honest with himself. He couldn't shake the déjà vu feeling as he watched Jessica run right through him. He wasn't as startled this time around. Within minutes she returned with her phone to her ear.

"Mum, thank god I got hold of you," Jessica said in a panic. She put her mum on speaker phone and placed it on the bathroom counter.

"What is it sweetheart?" Isabella asked trying to keep calm.

"You have to come over, it's Charlotte."

"What about Charlotte, is she okay?"

"God I don't know, she just started screaming in agony and collapsed on the bathroom floor."

"Why didn't you call the doctor?"

"I thought of you first because you used to be a nurse."

"I will be right there."

"Please hurry," said Jessica hanging up. She grabbed a wet flannel before sitting on the floor next to Charlotte's limp body. She ran the damp cloth over her friend's sweaty brow while she waited for her mum.

It wasn't long before the front door slammed shut and Isabella made her way to the bathroom. She crouched beside Jessica as she looked Charlotte over.

"What the hell happened?" Isabella asked her daughter.

"I don't know mum. She was going to have a bath and suddenly started screaming. I bolted in here and she collapsed."

"Grab her legs," Isabella said as she stood up.

"What?" Jessica asked looking confused.

"Grab her legs because we can't have her lying on this cold floor, even if she is in her dressing gown." Isabella lifted Charlotte under her arms while Jessica grabbed her ankles. "We'll take her to the lounge-room."

Jordan watched in agony as his mother and sister struggled to carry Charlotte to the lounge-room. He followed close behind, wishing he was able to help in some way. What could he do though, he was basically a ghost. A jolt of panic swept through him at that thought. Had Vincent just killed him? No, he couldn't think like that. He had already experienced this dream state, even if he didn't remember all the details.

"I'll go get some blankets," Isabella said. They had put Charlotte on the three seater leather settee to make her comfortable.

Jordan saw and felt his mother walk right through him. Why hadn't he gotten out of the way. He was pondering that thought when she stepped through him again.

"Jessica, when was the last time your brother was here?" she asked placing the blanket over Charlotte.

"Not for weeks.... why?"

"No reason," Isabella shrugged, she could swear he was in the room with them. Her worry over what was happening to him could be causing that. She could still feel the throbbing in her body. The call of the rose was still being sent out and since she wasn't being summoned just yet, she would stay and help Charlotte as best she could. "How long has she been sick?"

"Sick?" Jessica asked in confusion.

"Yes, sick."

"Well she's had no energy the past two or three days. We just thought it was a stomach bug. Why didn't Dad come with you?"

"He had to go away on some urgent business."

"Oh… how long will he be gone for?"

"Not that long, hopefully," she said giving her daughter a smile that didn't reach her eyes. She prayed with all her soul that her words were true.

Jordan saw the pained look on his mother's face. Could she possibly know what had happened to him? He didn't have time to ponder that thought, the feeling of being pulled away took him over and he disappeared from the room.

Chapter Thirty-Five

While driving up the long path to the house Richard didn't get the chance to take in the beauty of his surroundings. All he could focus on was the mystical call of the rose summoning him back to the other realm. He hadn't been trying to make his wife feel better. She did have a point. It was only the full blood elves that were being called, so she had to stay behind. Richard knew his wife though and as soon as the call eased enough to allow her access, she would make her way to the house. Until then she was stuck in the human realm.

As Richard pulled up in front of the house, he could see the rose on the front door. It was glowing black and looked like it was throbbing. Getting out of the car, he slowly walked up to the door. He placed his hand on the rose and closed his eyes. He called upon what little power his human form would allow and felt for any traces of his son. Richard opened his eyes feeling his son's pain, fear and anguish before opening the door. The house was in total darkness which was strange considering it was early afternoon and the place should have been flooded with daylight. Not giving it another thought he headed straight up stairs to his son's room.

Richard could feel the power from the other realm radiating from the mirror. Walking into the room, he had to shield his eyes from the glow that the mirror was casting. More proof that his son was in danger. Looking around he noticed the suitcases sitting next to the bed, still unpacked. He couldn't help feeling that the trouble Jordan was in was his fault. He hadn't prepared his son for going to the other realm. He hadn't even told him that the stories his grandmother told him as a child, were in fact all true. Jordan was destined to be king of all the elves. He had powers of his own, he just didn't know it yet. Richard looked down in shame. He had failed his son and in turn, failed his people. *Yet again.* What kind of a king did that make him he thought to himself as he walked towards the mirror?

Once he stood in front of the mirror he looked into it. He knew what would happen once he stepped through that glass. His human form would be gone and he would revert back to his former self. When he returned to the human realm the aging process would start again. That, he was not looking forward to. Especially if Isabella didn't join him in the other realm. Deciding he could delay no longer, he closed his eyes and stepped through.

It had been so long since Richard had stepped into the other realm. He had forgotten that it was like walking through a door on a submarine. There were a few tiny differences on the other side though. He could feel his elf form return. The narrowing of his eyes and the lengthening and pointing of his ears. The years he had aged in the human realm were being wiped away, as if he had never been there. He also felt his full power returning and he seemed to be stronger than he remembered. '*God, I missed that feeling,*' he thought to himself.

When he opened his eyes he saw a beautiful young elf, she looked more like a tall and slender pixie. Peter Pan was the first thing he thought of when he saw her. She was a foot shorter than he and had short black hair. Her silver eyes were like his and she was wearing what looked like green leggings and a matching V-neck top. The outfit looked to be made from velvet. He smiled at her even though she was standing there with her hands on her hips. She was tapping her foot and scowling at him.

"What took you so long?" she snapped while glaring at him and continuing to tap her foot.

"Is that any way to greet your king?" Richard asked her. She was one of the few elves who could get away with talking to him like that.

"Terribly sorry your majesty," she said sarcastically. She waved her hand and bowed in a very formal and exaggerated greeting.

"That's better......Now come here and give your big brother a hug," Richard said with a smile holding out his arms to her.

Smiling the young woman ran straight into his arms. She wrapped her arms around his waist and closed her eyes. She rested her head against his chest and squeezed her brother tight. "I missed you," she said.

"It's good to see you too," he said as he kissed the top of her head. He tightened his embrace, resting his check on her head.

Releasing his sister, he looked down at her. "What the hell is going on?" he asked her.

Pulling out of his arms she started to pace the room, talking very quickly as she did so. "It's Vincent… he has taken Jordan for his own means."

"Why would Vincent take my son?"

"To take his power and add it to his own," she said in a matter of fact tone "Now come on, we have to go," she said as she bolted towards the door.

"TRACEY STOP," yelled Richard.

She stopped instantly and slowly turned around to face her brother. "You know I hate being called Tracey."

"Well calling you Trixie wouldn't have the same effect at getting you to stop," Richard answered with a smile.

"Why did you stop me?" Trixie asked.

"Fools rush in where angels fear to tread."

"Stuff the bloody angels, your son is in danger. We have to go now," she insisted.

"Trixie, I am aware of that. However, it will do no one any good if we were to go in there with guns blazing. Yes, I want to go and save my son. If I have to kill that worthless brother of ours to do it, then so help me I will. Rushing in there with no plan or background of the situation could get us both killed and I don't fancy that happening. Don't forget I've not been here in thirty years. I need to catch up on what has happened, so I can decide on what action to take," Richard replied seriously. He motioned for his sister to sit down on the bed. "Now tell me, what the hell has been happening since I've been away."

"Where would you like me to start?" Trixie said as she walked over and sat down.

"Tracey." Richard said glaring at his sister.

"Fine," Trixie said with exasperation. "Not long after you went to the human realm to be with Isabella, Vincent decided that he should and would take your place as king. I guess he figured with you gone, it was his right."

"Why? Because he is the next one down from me. It doesn't work that way. Not to mention that he doesn't have the power to be a king. Never mind The King," Richard said in frustration.

"That didn't matter to him. You weren't here and he wanted to rule. He wanted to have the power that you have. He was not a happy camper when he found he didn't get that power. The situation got worse once he discovered he could take powers. I'm guessing that since he has never tried to take mine, or anybody else whose absence would have been noticed he knew that it would summon you back here," Trixie explained.

"Ok then," Richard said. He wasn't at all surprised by his sister's words. Vincent had always done what was best for Vincent and damn anyone else. "So what does he want with my son?"

"His power," Trixie said.

"But Jordan doesn't know he has any power, let alone how to use it."

"Exactly and Vincent knows this," Trixie said tapping her lips in deep thought. "I could feel how powerful Jordan is. His powers are out of control because he had no knowledge of them." Trixie noticed the look of shame cross her brothers face and she put her hand on his arm. "Richard, it's not your fault."

"Whose fault is it then? My son has been taken by a power hungry lunatic for the powers I should have told him about and taught him how to use," Richard replied in anger.

Trixie stood up and faced her brother, she pointed her finger at him.

"Richard Jonathan Elfin, now you listen to me and you listen good. I know exactly what you are thinking. You did not fail your son or your people. Your people knew why you went to the human realm. They understood and at the time many would have done the same if they were in your shoes.

"As for your son, it was Jordan who decided to go to the house and not heed his mother's word in staying away. It was a complete accident that he arrived here too soon. He was not meant to find out about this place for at least another two weeks. Which in turn, you would have been preparing for. So don't you dare sit there and start feeling sorry for yourself or dwell in self-pity. I don't care that you are king of the elves, you are my big brother and I will have no problems with smacking the crap out of you for thinking such things." When Trixie finished she nodded her head to finalise her words. She meant business but she also knew she couldn't actually smack anything out of her brother. But it wouldn't stop her trying.

Richard looked at his sister in stunned silence, like he always did when she had an outburst like that. It happened so rarely that it always shocked him. He mulled over her words and one thing she said suddenly hit him. "How do you know he got here accidently? I don't recall mentioning it."

"I just happened to be in here when he arrived, that and he also told me. His entrance was rather dramatic," replied Trixie sheepishly.

"Did you teach him how to use the communication mirror?" he asked and Trixie nodded. "Jordan told his mother that a servant girl had helped him," Richard said completely confused.

"I kind of gave him that impression."

"Why?"

"The poor sod had just fallen through a mirror into another realm. He knew nothing about this world and to find a pixie looking elf staring at him startled him a bit. What was I to say? Hey, I'm your long lost aunt you know nothing about? He was in shock as it was and thought he was dreaming. I didn't want to add any more confusion to that. In addition, I suspected he would start asking questions and I didn't feel it was my place to answer them so I let him think I was a servant girl. I showed him how to use the mirror so he could speak to either you or Isabella when he wanted to. Didn't I mention all that crap to you when we spoke while Jordan was here?"

"No you didn't and you told nobody he was here?" Richard asked, knowing how it sounded.

"No, I didn't tell anyone," Trixie said while looking at her brother and wanting to slap him. "I know you love me and had to ask, so don't you dare insult me by saying it now."

"How the hell did Vincent know he was here. How was he able to take him?"

"Vincent would have sensed his arrival. The power flowing from Jordan was coming off him in waves. It would have been like a homing beacon." Trixie looked at her brother with shame in her silver eyes. "After Jordan received a visit from Vincent, the next morning I brought him into the garden so he could have a little time to process everything. I only left him for a few minutes because I didn't think anything like this would happen," she said as the tears started to fall.

Richard walked over and pulled his sister into a tight embrace. "It's not your fault. You were only thinking of Jordan and his best interests. You didn't know our brother was going to take him." Richard cupped his sisters face in his hands and wiped away her tears. "Vincent is not an idiot. He has always been sly and devious. If he wanted Jordan badly enough, he would have got him regardless. As luck would have it, an opportunity presented itself to him and he took it. Jordan being in the dark about his powers allowed Vincent to take full advantage. But I never thought he would do anything like this to his family."

"His lust for power has corrupted him. He doesn't care how he gets it or who he hurts in the process."

Richard raised an eyebrow at his sister, recreating a scene from Star Wars in his head. "His lust for power?"

"Yeah, like Anakin in Star Wars. His lust for power turns him to the dark side."

"Anakin," Richard said looking at her blankly. He should have known she would be a Star Wars fan.

"Are you telling me you have been in the human realm for years and have never heard of Star Wars?" Trixie asked in shock.

He enjoyed his sister's reactions. She had always been able to lighten his mood, no matter the situation. He decided to go along with the pretence. He had seen the films and remembered a favourite scene featuring Princess Leia wearing a gold bikini.

Richard shook his head at his sister and smiled, "Come on, we have a corrupt brother to find. We need to show him his actions have consequences," he said as they walked towards the door.

Chapter Thirty-Six

On the way to his war room he had to go through his old office. He was not surprised to find his trusted generals Martouf, Lantash and Mattias waiting for him. After the usual greetings were made, they got down to business. He wasn't surprised when Martouf sat behind his desk,

"Cheeky bastard," Richard murmured humorously. His words were directed at Martouf.

"What, did you want this seat?" Martouf replied with a grin.

"No, it's fine, I'm too anxious to sit any way," Richard replied. He looked around his office, everything looked the same. The mahogany desk, the big brown leather chair behind it were like a glimpse of the past. A brown three seater settee sat by the fire place. Various pictures were hanging on the wall in dark wooden frames. He watched as Lantash and Mattias took seats on the settee. Trixie stood next to him.

"Right," Martouf said clapping his hands and rubbing them together. "Let's get down to business, when are we going to get your son back?"

"We? I don't need any help to retrieve my son," Richard said with authority.

"Oh your so right." Everyone locked their gazes on Martouf, who was now sitting casually at Richard's desk. His feet were resting on the desk one ankle over the other. He was using a dagger to clean his finger nails. He lifted his eyes from what he was doing and noticed everyone staring at him. "What? It's a fact," he finished with a shrug.

"What are you saying," asked Trixie who was clearly panicked.

"Think about it…. Richard is King of the Elves, the rightful king I might add. Therefore, he is the most powerful elf in the realm. He could easily go to Vincent's castle and wipe everyone out, without any real effort on his part. Plus, the fact the only elves at the autumn castle who know Richard are Lampros and Vincent. All the elves at Vincent's castle are young-ones. Elves that were too young to remember you or have been born since you left and went to the Human Realm. In their eyes Vincent is the king and they would gladly fight to the death for him," Martouf concluded.

"So, you're in agreement with me?" Richard asked. He wasn't sure if he was asking a question or making a statement.

"Oh absolutely," Martouf replied smirking. "Go off to the castle and take all the young elves out. The best warrior that Vincent has is Lampros. We know he won't go against you, which for me is a good thing because I really don't fancy having to kill my cousin. So, Trixie can go with you to keep him busy just in case." A snort from Trixie grabbed Martouf's attention. "Trixie sweetheart the sooner you stop being so stubborn and get with Lampros the bloody better." He gave her a smile and a wink before turning back to face Richard. "So my King, what do you think of that plan?"

"Perfect, Trixie and I will leave within the hour," he said as he made to leave.

"Oh, one more thing," said Martouf.

"What," Richard snapped at his head general.

"What if one of the young-ones gets a lucky shot?"

"What," Richard asked with confusion on his face.

"What if one of the young-ones gets a lucky shot with an arrow before you reach the castle? I mean Trixie can hold her own, but not against a barrage of arrow's."

"We would both be dead," Richard replied without emotion.

"Lampros wouldn't let anything happen to me," Trixie said with a quiver in her voice.

"Your right he wouldn't, however Vincent would contradict any orders Lampros would give. Best friend or not, I wouldn't doubt for a second that Vincent would take Lampros out before Lampros got to him. And then what? The King would be dead. His power would automatically be transferred to Jordan. Who in turn wouldn't know what was happening to him never mind knowing how to use the powers. Then what's to stop Vincent from gutting him while he is chained to a wall or something. Vincent would then be the king like he wishes to be and we would all be fucked."

"You're a bastard," was Richard's only response.

"I'm just saying it like it is, you are not infallible. One lucky shot and it's over." Martouf said as he moved to sit in the chair properly with his hands on the desk.

"You win," said Richard in defeat. He looked around the room at Trixie, Mattias, Lantash and Martouf. "War room now," he ordered as he stalked out of the room.

Chapter Thirty-Seven

Richard walked into the war room, with Trixie at his heels. She wasn't usually allowed inside, because she was female. Only the men were warriors and allowed in the war room. Even though having two big brothers, Richard knew Trixie could hold her own in battle. She would indeed make a good warrior, maybe it was time for a change.

Richard watched his sister taking in her surroundings. She was like a kid in a candy store.

"Has it always looked like this?" Trixie asked.

Richard looked around the room. Stone grey walls decorated with colourful banners, showing each general's crest. Stained glass windows and a military tactical map table in the centre. "Yep," he said looking at his sister.

"It's so medieval," she replied.

Richard couldn't argue, the whole room looked like something out of the human history books. To be fair, they were built at the same time. The room hadn't changed since his great grandfather and his ancestors ruled before him.

Heading over to the map, he got a clear view of what the land looked like. The map was the only thing in the room that got constantly undated. He really didn't need to look at the map since he knew the layout of the land well because they weren't currently at war with anyone.

"So what do we know?" Richard asked.

"Vincent has your son," Lampros said as he entered the room. He walked straight to Richard, bowed and kneeled. "Your majesty."

"Lampros what are you doing here?" Richard asked motioning for him to stand. "Shouldn't you be with Vincent?"

"Technically. Although, I am honour and duty bound to serve the king. Once the call was sent out, I knew you would be returning."

"Vincent will call you a traitor, with you being his general and all."

"Which is why I can't dally and must get back before I am missed. I just came to give you the heads up."

"Which is?"

"Jordan is being kept in the dungeon."

"I searched the dungeon and there was nobody there, only that necklace." Trixie said.

"What necklace?" Richard asked looking down at his sister.

"You know, the cursed one," she said absently.

"It was on the floor, in the middle of an empty dungeon?" Richard clarified.

"Yes," Trixie and Lampros said at the same time.

"Mother fucker," Richard said realising what his brother was doing. "Lampros."

"Yes your majesty."

"You get back to the Autumn Elves castle. It would be best if you don't hear any plans we make. Not because I don't trust you, but if you don't know anything then Vincent can't use it to his advantage."

"Yes your majesty," Lampros replied as he bowed and made to leave. He turned to look at Martouf. "Later cous."

"Lampros," Martouf said while smiling at his younger cousin leaving the room. He turned to Richard and continued, "So what's the plan?"

Richard started pacing, getting his thoughts together. He stopped suddenly and turned to face his generals. "Mattias."

"Yes your majesty" Mattias said standing to attention.

"You can still flash can't you?"

"Yes," he answered raising an eyebrow.

"Good, go and get me Ruby," he ordered. He was finally in king mode.

"Yes your majesty," and with that, he flashed out of the room.

"Lantash gather our troops, and assemble them in the court yard."

"Yes your majesty," he said before bowing and leaving the room.

"Richard, why didn't you ask Lampros if Jordan was still alive? I mean the call has activated," said Martouf.

"I don't need to, I can feel that my son is alive and in pain. His powers are rejuvenating as we speak."

"Rejuvenating," Trixie and Martouf said in unison.

"Yes, there is no other explanation. My son should be dead with no powers at all, but I can sense different. Everyone else has died when Vincent has forcefully taken their powers from them from what I understand. I guess that Jordan has a little leeway, being heir to the throne. Although, I suspect that he would only be able to go through it so many times before it actually does kill him. Do you know what will happen shortly after that?" he said while looking at Trixie, who just shook her head. "Vincent will soon be following him."

Mattias returned to the room with a protesting Ruby and caught everyone's attention.

"Ah, Ruby," Richard said.

Spinning around at the sound of his voice Ruby's eyes landed on Richard. "Your majesty," she said while holding her long red velvet dress at the sides as she curtsied. She looked around the room and noticed that it was only the old crew and there were no newbies. "Richard when did you get back?"

"When do you think?"

"So snide, what's with the attitude," she snapped.

"Did you put a spell on my son?"

"Straight to the point, I can do that and yes I did."

"What was the spell?"

"Exactly what Vincent requested of course. He asked for it to be only him to see and sense Jordan. He basically wanted to shield him from Trixie." She glanced towards Trixie, "You would have been able to hear and feel him but if it counts for anything he won't be shielded any longer."

"But your spells last for ages, why wouldn't Jordan be shielded now?" Trixie asked.

"Because I know what Vincent has become. I knew if provoked enough, he would do the young man harm. I also knew who the young man was, so I deliberately put a time limit on the spell. I told Vincent the spell would be broken once the king returned."

"I love you sometimes," Richard said. He walked over too Ruby and embraced her. "Thank you for that," he said as he placed a kiss on her forehead.

"Do you need me for anything else?"

"No. Mattias, could you please escort Ruby back to where you acquired her from."

"Yes your majesty," he said grabbing Ruby's hand and flashing from the room.

"What the hell was that about?" Trixie asked with her hands on her hips.

"Call it a hunch," Richard said as he started pacing the room. He was waiting for Mattias' return and trying to decide what he should do next. He looked at his sister thinking he didn't really want to bring her into what could potentially turn into a blood bath. It wouldn't be long before his wife returned either. Doing the only thing he could, he got out his communication device and opened it. "Christina of the Fae."

"What?" Snapped a voice behind him.

He jumped and spun around to find his mother-in -law standing there smiling at him.

"Did I make the big Elf King jump," she snickered.

"You did that deliberately," he snapped.

"Yep…now what can I do for you, Your Majesty," she said giving him a little bow.

"I need you to meet your daughter when she arrives. Bring her to the Autumn Elf castle to collect Jordan. If Vincent does a runner, then I will need to go after him. I hear he has been stealing Fae powers and I may need you to flash me to where he is."

"You do realise that my daughter can flash or did you forget again."

"I forgot. But do you seriously think she will leave Jordan's side?"

"Good point.... Consider it done Your Majesty," she said before bowing and flashing from the room.

"Right, start heading out to the court yard. I will join you shortly," Richard said once Mattias returned. After everyone had left the room, he turned in the opposite direction, heading towards his living quarters. He needed to make sure he was in the appropriate clothing for the realm.

Chapter Thirty-Eight

Richard walked out the wooden double doors to the large court yard. He could feel the stone cobbles through the thin soles of his shoes. After spending thirty years in jeans, he did feel a bit stupid being in tights and a tunic. If Trixie looked like Peter Pan he was a dead ringer for Robin Hood right down to the hat, which did nothing to hide his pointed ears.

The sun beat down on his face as he shifted his quiver and bow onto his shoulder. He hadn't been back in thirty years and now that he was he was dragging his men off to battle. He really didn't want anyone getting hurt or possibly killed, but Martouf had been right.

One lucky shot and it could all be over. He could hear his men talking as he approached them.

"All hail king Richard," a few voices called out as he came into view. He couldn't help but feel pride as he looked over the crowed of elves on bended knee. Richard smiled and bowed slightly to the crowed using his hands to motion for them to stand. Any of them that knew him well enough, knew he hated all the formal crap that went with his title. He was just one of the guys, always had been.

"My fellow elves, how are we all?"

"Anxiously awaiting orders to retrieve our prince your majesty," one elf responded. The army of elves around them nodded their agreement.

"Zydek, it's been a long time," Richard said walking up to the older elf who had served under his father. He grabbed his forearm in a manly shake.

"Yes it has young-one."

"So what's the plan, your majesty?" yelled another from some-where in the crowd.

Richard backed up so he had a good view of everyone present. "Since I have been away for so long, I wouldn't feel right if I didn't give you the chance to decide. Yes, my son is your prince and the next king. However, he has grown up in the human realm and none of you know him. So I give you the option to withdraw from this battle if you so choose."

"Your Majesty we know the risks, now what's the plan?" said Zydek.

"We will all gather in the autumn forest. From there I will head to the castle to get my son back peacefully…."

"But your majesty," Martouf interrupted.

"No, that's my call. If things go tits up, then you guys will be in the forest for back up." Looking over the crowd he continued, "Mattias."

"Yes your majesty."

"If one of the young-ones should cause my death this day then you will flash into that bloody castle and get my son, or I'll haunt the fuck out of you. Got it."

"Yes your majesty," Mattias said smiling.

"Everyone I would usually say you have an hour to get geared up, but it looks like you already are. Head home, spend some time with your loved ones and we will head out in an hour." With a clap of his hands, everyone dispersed.

Chapter Thirty-Nine

An hour and a half later Richard stood under the trees at the edge of the Autumn Elves castle grounds with Martouf on his right side and Lantash on his left. Mattias was not far back from them leaning against a tree, arming his cross bow.

"Where is my sister?" Richard asked Martouf as he looked around for her.

"She said she had something she had to do," Martouf said shrugging.

"Oh okay then." That knowledge gave him some small relief from the urge he was fighting within himself to just storm the castle. He had to use his head and try as best as he could to control his emotions. Turning around, he addressed the crowded forest.

"Right, plan A is about to commence. I will say this, I don't know how many of the young-ones are your children and I would ask you to spare their lives if you can. They are following orders as they should. Unfortunately, they believe Vincent to be the king which I blame myself for as I wasn't here to prove different. The call of the rose will also have them confused no doubt, but by all means, disarm the little shits and may the spirits of the elders be with us."

Turning Richard emerged from the trees and headed down the long cobbled path towards to castle gates. Hands behind his back he acted as if he hadn't a care in the world. He could see in the distance the paths that led to the villages. They were abandoned after the battle of the realms and lush grass went right up to the level of the surrounding forest.

"Halt who goes there?"

Richard raised his eyebrows at the two young elves brandishing swords. Did they really just say that? Well two could play that game.

"Would you believe King Richard back from the crusades." He couldn't help snickering at the confused looks on their faces. One of the guards stepped forward.

"There is no King Richard."

"Whatever. Tell Vincent that I have come for my son."

"King Vincent is busy. I don't know who you are, but you will show respect to our king and address His Majesty accordingly."

"I would if he was," Richard said taking a step toward the young elf while resisting the urge to use his powers and swat them both like flies. He stopped abruptly as he felt the point of the sword in his chest. Looking down at the blade he asked, "What is your name?"

"Iolaus sir," the young elf answered not removing his sword.

"Well Iolaus, I'm sure your king and your parents would be proud of your actions today. Would you kindly tell my younger brother that I stopped by and will be returning to collect my son, by force if need be," he said as he turned to leave.

"Who is your brother sir?"

"Your apparent king," he said waving his hand as he headed down the path.

Chapter Forty

Vincent ran into the cell panicked. He had seen his brother heading towards the castle and knew it wouldn't be a good thing with him walking away. Actually he was surprised his brother hadn't just barged into the castle. Richard must be being diplomatic or very calm, Vincent thought to himself. He had heard what his brother had said to the elves that guarded the gate. A calm Richard was much worse than a rampaging one and the panic that Vincent was currently feeling in the pit of his stomach was warranted.

Raising the chains his nephew was bound in, a satisfied smile creased his face as he watched his unconscious nephews body being dragged off the cell floor. He had no feelings of remorse for what he had done. Even with the fear he had of his brother. What was done, was done. His nephew looked so much like his brother. He still felt nothing when he noticed the blood running down his nephews forearms from the shackles at his wrist. Taking his powers while he had been chained in metal had probably not been the best idea. It had amplified the effect of it.

Shrugging, Vincent raised his hand to take more of Jordan's powers. If his brother was going to kill him for what he had done, Vincent figured he might as well make it worth it and get all the extra power he could. He stopped abruptly at the sound of someone clearing their throat and glanced in that direction.

"Lampros, what the hell are you doing in here?"

Lampros raised his arms from where he sat by the wall, showing him the shackles he had been put in.

"Why the hell are you in shackles?" Vincent asked raising his brows.

"Your loyal subjects arrested me for treason."

"Why for treason?"

"I may have said you weren't the king a few too many times. So they arrested me," he said shrugging.

"And you let them?"

"I decided to sit this one out, besides only the king can pardon one of his loyal subjects once they have been arrested for treason." Looking more closely at Vincent he continued, "Why do you seem a little panicked?"

"Richard is here," Vincent said while stopping the chains that were raising his nephew.

"I know. I could hear him. So what are you doing in here?"

"I need a power boost," he said moving closer to his nephew. "Especially if I'm going to be facing my too calm big brother."

"You're going to take more of his powers? That could kill him, hell, I'm surprised it didn't the first time." Vincent's eyes were filled with greed, which told Lampros there would be no getting through to his friend. "You will be lucky if Richard doesn't kill you."

"I might as well make my death worth it," Vincent sneered placing his fingertips near his nephew's chest.

Electric lightning bolts shot out from his finger tips and into his nephew. Jordan's powers were like a drug to Vincent and he wanted to stay on this high forever. The sound of Jordan screaming in agony was music to his ears as the euphoric feeling of his power washed over his entire body.

Richard hadn't even made it half way down the path towards the forest before he heard his son's screams and could feel his pain as if it was his own. Anger surged through his body so strong there was nothing he could do to stop the power bursting from his hands. Spinning on his heal he directed the lightning bolts towards the castle, causing small explosions along the castle wall. Big chunks of stone wall fell to the ground, narrowly missing the elves positioned below. A red hot rage had set in, like nothing Richard had ever felt before. His brother was going to be one sorry son of a bitch, once he was through with him.

A sudden jolt to his left shoulder stopped his attack abruptly. He flew back and landed as pain shot through his shoulder on impact. Looking down he noticed he had been shot, just as Martouf and Lantash arrived at his side.

"Mother fucker, who gave them fucking guns?" Richard said between gritted teeth.

"The king is down…. Charge!"

Richard closed his eyes as he heard the order. He didn't know who gave the order. All he could do was watch as the other elves emerged from the forest running straight for the castle with their swords out. They charged straight past them and the ground was vibrating around them with each step.

Glancing at the castle, Martouf could see that the walls had now become unstable. The archers on the battlement wouldn't be up there long before it collapsed, but it still gave them enough time to fire their weapons.

"Shit." He turned quickly and kneeled next to Richard. "Richard. Shields," Martouf ordered. He placed pressure on the wound in Richards shoulder. Richard hissed with pain as a barrage of arrows came heading their way.

Chapter Forty-One

"Richard put your fucking shields up," Martouf yelled in a panic as the arrows headed their way. His personal shield wasn't big enough to cover the three of them. Lantash only had his gauntlets on his forearms to protect him, as he fought with his Sai daggers.

Richard had only just activated his shields as the arrows reached them. They struck the shield and dropped to the ground around them. He could hear the chinking of swords connecting as his loyal elves fought against the younger elves. They didn't know who he was which was a situation he would soon rectify and mistake he would not make again.

"That was close," Lantash said letting out a sigh of relief. He watched in horror as a big chunk of castle wall came tumbling to the ground taking elves with it. "You did a good job of remodelling the castle."

"Shut up," Richard snapped as he slowly stood up, clutching his injured shoulder. "You know what we are missing right now?"

"No," Martouf and Lantash said together.

"A bloody medic, all our powers and we don't even have power healing abilities." More arrows hit his shield, making Richard flinch. "This is bullshit, we are sitting ducks here and there is nowhere to take cover. Our armour is not designed to go against guns." The few elves who had the guns clearly didn't know how to use them. Whoever shot him, really did get a lucky shot the bastard.

"Well, we are pretty safe," Lantash said while running his hand over the shimmering shield.

Richard glared at Lantash. "*We are,* only because of my shield, but everybody else isn't." He looked around at the battle taking place. He un-sheathed his rapier knowing his bow and arrows would be useless with his injured arm. He wouldn't be able to carry his shield even if he had it with him and couldn't fight with his force field up anyway.

He noticed a few young-ones charging up the path towards them. Their swords were out ready to fight. Richard shook his head, raised an eyebrow and glanced over to the castle. He noticed that all the archers had gone, they must have fallen when the wall did.

"Stuff it," he said removing his force field. He took up a fighting stance, waiting for when they finally did reach them. Why should he tire himself out going to them?

Richard raised his sword in front of his face as the young-one Iolaus tried to bring his sword down on his head. Blocking that move, Richard swung the blade around, knocking the sword out of Iolaus' hand with one smooth move. He used the hilt of his sword to smack Iolaus on the head, knocking him out cold.

"Who the hell trained these men to fight, they are weaklings," he yelled as another elf came charging towards him.

"Lampros trained them, but you are right they have never seen battle before," Martouf replied. He swung his broad sword to avoid being thrust in the gut by the second young-one.

"What! Not even mock ones?" Richard asked exasperated as another one came heading his way.

"Nope, no battle scenarios. Just the basic training."

"These are lambs sent to slaughter." Richards words were emphasised when the Elf charging him tripped and fell flat on his face. His sword was knocked from his hand.

"Yep, considering who they are up against," Martouf said. He hit the young elf he was duelling with, with the hilt of his sword, knocking him out as well. "Lantash, what the hell are you doing?"

"What?" Lantash asked as he looked up from cleaning his nails with his weapons. "There were three of us, two who were charging at once and they went to you two. I don't even need my weapons for this fight one punch and I would knock these little shits out. Even if they are carrying swords."

"I don't have time for this shit," Richard murmured as he sheathed his sword. He turned and headed back down the path towards the castle. He noticed a few young elves heading their way and raised his hand in a move worthy of any Sith Lord and sent the elves flying back across the castle grounds. Maybe he was a bit too forceful. They were flung over the other elves fighting and hit the forest trees. Richard flinched, he hadn't meant to do that.

Reaching the front doors of the castle he came face to face with a young elf holding his sword up. He couldn't have been more than sixteen years old. Richard could see the terrified look on the young-one's face, never mind the fact the kid was physically shaking. "Move or I will move you."

"Richard," Martouf yelled.

"What," he yelled back not taking his eyes off the young elf. The sound of sword fights could be heard around him. Richard guessed the bullets must of ran out.

"Don't hurt him," Martouf said as he reached Richards side. "Nicodemus stand down."

"Why?" The young elf asked defiantly.

"Because I am ordering you to do so."

"But Dad this man is not the King and cousin Lampros has already been arrested for treason against King Vincent. Don't make me arrest you too."

"I'd like to see you try." Martouf said looking at his son. Lifting his leg, he kicked the sword out of his son's hand and grabbing him in a head lock before he had chance to do anything. "Richard go get your son."

Richard didn't need to be told twice, he headed through the castle door.

Chapter Forty-Two

Isabella stood in her son's bedroom at rose manor. She didn't really want to leave Charlotte in agony but she had very little choice. The call of the rose was now summoning her and if her instincts were correct, getting to Jordan would be the only thing that would help Charlotte. It was a shame that she still had a few years to go until she would know for certain.

She walked towards the glowing mirror and could barely see her reflection, due to the thin swirling mist in the glass. Rubbing her hands down her white blouse and jeans she closed her eyes and stepped through.

Isabella could feel her body begin to change the second she emerged on the other side. Being born in the human realm her features wouldn't change unlike that of her husbands, but it was a strange feeling none the less. Tingles washed through her body like she had pins and needles all over the place. It was a peculiar sensation as her body started reversing the aging process. The tightening of her face as the few wrinkles she did have were banished. The sagginess of her bum and breasts erased as she felt them lift back into the shape they were before she had had children. She couldn't believe she still remembered the feel of how her body had once been and couldn't help sweeping her hands over her arse and grabbing her boobs. The whole thing reminded her of the film, 'Death Becomes Her,' after the character had taken the potion.

Opening her eyes finally, she noticed the raised eyebrow on her mother's face. Smiling she let go of her breasts and hugged her mother, before turning to Trixie and doing the same.

"So, did you finished groping yourself?" Trixie asked with humour in her voice.

"It's weird, I feel like I did before I had Jordan and the girls."

"Well technically."

"Stretch marks! Do you think they have gone?" Isabella said as she started to lift her blouse to view her stomach.

"Isabella!" Christina couldn't believe that she would have to put up with her twenty-five-year-old daughter again. The first time was enough. She just might kill Vincent herself.

"What," Isabella said as she pulled her blouse back down over her jeans. She looked at her white plimsolls she was wearing and wished she had on a pair of short heeled boots. Maybe she should go back and get some. She turned back to the mirror but she didn't make it very far before Trixie blocked her way.

"Isabella what the hell are you doing?" her mother asked.

"Going to get my heeled boots," she said as she turned to face her mother.

"Why?"

"Because they would go better with this outfit," she said motioning to her attire.

"She's right, they would," Trixie said in agreement.

"Trixie," said Christina glaring at the elf. "Do not encourage her, for god sake."

"Is this memory loss thing common?" Trixie asked over Isabella's head.

"Did Richard have memory loss, when he came through?"

"No, he was fine," Trixie said with a shrug.

"It might be because she was born in the human realm, I just don't know. We will just have to give her a few minutes. Her fifty-five-year-old self needs to catch up with the younger body or whatever the hell it's doing." Christina held the bridge of her nose, she didn't know what to do or what had happened. If anything like this had ever happened before, it was before her time. Even when the battle of the realms was taking place, the call of the rose hadn't been set off. Likely due to the fact that everyone had been summoned back before the battle started.

Isabella tilted her head to look at her mother. A jolt of energy shot through her, sending her backwards into Trixie and almost sending both women back through the mirror.

"Oh my god…. Jordan." Isabella said wide-eyed as she righted herself. She could feel that her son was in pain, who the hell was hurting him? "Where the hell is my son?" It was as if the jolt had knocked her senses back into action.

Trixie and Christina both looked at each other.

"Mother…. Trixie…. who is currently hurting my son and why the hell didn't I feel it in the human realm?"

"In answer to your second question, it was because you were in the human realm," Christina told her flatly.

"And my first question?" she asked raising her eyebrows and looking between her mother and sister-in-law. Her mother had a blank look on her face but Trixie's whole body screamed out she knew something. "Trixie," said Isabella. She heard her mumble something but didn't quite catch it. "Sorry, what?"

"Vincent."

"Vincent what?" Isabella looked at her sister-in-law with confusion.

Trixie lifted her head and looked Isabella in the eye. "Vincent is the one hurting your son."

"As in our Vincent?"

"Yep."

"Why the hell would he hurt my son? His nephew?" Isabella was gob-smacked. She couldn't believe what she was hearing.

"Vincent has become power hungry and wants to be king."

"But in order for him to be king, Rich…." A horrible thought stopped her mid-sentence. "Can Vincent forcefully take powers?"

"Yes, usually the person ends up dead afterwards though."

"Mother fucker," Isabella said as she stormed towards the bedroom door.

"Isabella where are you going," Trixie asked heading after her.

"I'm going to get my son and with luck stop the demise of my husband in the process."

"But you don't know where he is."

Isabella closed her eyes, not sensing anything she looked at the two women. "Can either of you sense my son or husband?" Both women shook their heads. "Right, well we are going to assume that your second eldest brother is stupid enough to keep my son in his castle."

"And if he's not there?" Trixie and Christina asked together.

"Then I will pull every single god damn realm apart until I find my son and god help any Elf, Fae or Witch who gets in my way." With those last words Isabella stormed out of the room.

"I'm so proud of my daughter sometimes," Christina said to herself as she and Trixie hurried after Isabella.

Reaching the edge of the dark forest surrounding Autumn Elves castle, Isabella had to rest against a tree to catch her breath, man was she unfit.

"Shit," she said slapping her forehead.

"What is it dear?" her mother asked her placing a hand on her shoulder.

"I can flash."

"I know you can," said Christina looking at her daughter in confusion.

"I power walked through a bloody forest and two realms when I could have just flashed straight to my son. God damn it." Isabella kicked the nearest tree in frustration. "Fuck that hurt," she said as she grabbed her foot. She hissed through her teeth when the pain shot up her leg.

"I wish you would stop swearing, you sound like your twenty-five again." Christina hated hearing the foul language coming out of her daughters' mouth. She was glad when that phased had past the first time.

"But I am twenty-five again," she said as she put her foot down slowly. The pain had subsided thankfully. "Thanks to my good for nothing brother-in-law who just had to kidnap my son and put his life in danger." The tone of her voice was getting more high pitched with every word, she was clearly going into hysterics. "Which in turn set off the call of the rose, which then resets everyone's age who have had no choice but to come back to the realm and - "

SLAP!

Isabella's hand went to her stinging cheek. She looked at her mother who was standing there with her hands on her hips staring straight at her.

"Thank you for that mother," Isabella gritted out through clenched teeth. Her face still stinging.

"Your welcome. Now that you've had your little hysterical fit, are we ready to go?"

Isabella looked towards the castle and she could see elves everywhere. They were either fighting or lying on the ground. Dropping her hands to her sides she felt within herself for her powers, she had a feeling she was going to need them.

"Yes! Come on," she said taking a step forward.

"You're not going to flash?" Trixie asked.

"No, anyone come's near me and I will zap the bastard. Now let's go," she said taking a step out of the forest. Trixie and her mother were beside her as they made their way down the path. All three women stopped in their tracks once they got a good view of the castle.

The top half of the castle was on the floor. At least one side of it was a big pile of stone rubble. Had someone used a bomb in the place? Isabella couldn't tell but she was pretty sure they didn't have anything like that in the Elven Realm. She glanced over the damaged rooms, but could tell that the dungeons had been left alone. She breathed a sigh of relief. She didn't know why but she had a feeling that was where Jordan was being kept.

She continued towards the castle but stopped when a war cry sounded behind her. Spinning on her heels she saw a young elf running towards them with his sword in the air. Panicking, Isabella sent a bolt of light straight at him. He flew through the air and landed on his arse. The stunned look on his face would have made her laugh had she not been preoccupied with getting to her son. Thank god she had only stunned him, he looked no older than her daughter Joanne.

She continued towards the castle as an explosion ripped the air. It came from inside the castle and sent more of the wall crashing to the ground. Jumping from the initial shock of the explosion, she decided to wait until the dust had settled before scanning the damage.

When the dust settled enough for her to see she scanned the damage and froze. She hadn't even realised that she had stopped breathing until she gulped down a massive breath of air. The dungeon area this time had been damaged. The hole in the wall wasn't big enough to see clearly but she could see that someone was by the wall. She couldn't tell who it was though.

"Lampros," Trixie screamed when she saw the elf through the hole in the dungeon wall. She suddenly took off running towards the castle.

Trixie's outburst had given Isabella her answer.

"Ah fuck," Isabella breathed out just before taking off after Trixie with her mother close behind. She just hoped the castle wall wouldn't come crashing down before they all got out.

Chapter Forty-Three

"Jesus Richard watch where your firing those things," Lampros yelled after ducking a fire bolt that sent the wall to the dungeon crashing to the floor below. There was not going to be any castle left by the time he was done.

Richard sent an apologetic smile in Lampros' direction. He turned briefly towards his son, who was still hanging limply by the chains his brother had tied him with. Tightening the grip, he had on his brother's shirt front, he looked at his brother. He couldn't help the smile that crossed his face at the fear in his brother's eyes. Yes, Vincent was a sneaky, conniving, crafty bastard, but he was still shit scared of his big brother.

Richard and Vincent had been using their powers to fight each other down the long corridor until Vincent disappeared into one of the cells. Richard finally made it to the dungeon cell and caught his brother trying to steel even more of his son's power.

Richard had been attempting not to hit his son or Lampros as they continued with their power battle. Vincent didn't seem to care if he hit anyone or was in too much of a panic to not get hit since he was sending bolts flying all over the place. It was only when Richard had taken out most of the wall and almost Lampros with it, did he decide that enough was enough and grabbed his brother. Clenching his fist, he laid into his brother's face, punch after punch. Richard didn't even notice the blood on his knuckles or Vincent's face as he continued to punch out his rage.

It was only when he heard his wife shriek his name did he finally stop pounding into his face. He turned his attention to his wife who was standing by the dungeon door with her hands over her face.

Vincent used that opportunity to strike his brother in the throat and Richard instantly released him. He clutched his throat, struggling to breath as Vincent fled out the door almost knocking the three women flying.

Taking a quick look at her brother, Trixie headed straight for Lampros still chained up by the wall. Christina went to check on Richard while Isabella's main concern was her son. As she reached him she did the typical motherly thing and patted him down, checking to make sure he had nothing broken. Relief swamped her as she realised her son was still alive and breathing. She noticed the blood on his arms and she followed the trail finding badly blistered wounds around his wrists. The shackles were still cutting into them. Cursing she looked at her husband.

The torn look on his face almost broke her heart. She could tell he wanted to make sure their son was fine, but also go after his brother. The anger that surged through her at what Vincent had done to her son overrode all other senses.

"Go," she told him sternly. Richard blew her a kiss as he ran from the room.

"He'll be fine," her mother said as she stood next to her, placing a comforting hand on her shoulder.

"Jordan," Isabella patted her son's face trying to wake him up. "Jordan."

Jordan scrunched up his face at the pain of someone slapping him. He felt like he had been run over by a double decker bus. His whole body ached. Slowly opening his eyes his heart dropped to his stomach as he looked into the eyes of his grandmother. "Good god, I'm dead."

Chapter Forty-Four

Richard reached the castle gate rubbing at his throat where his brother had hit him. He glanced around for any sign of him.

"Richard," Mattias yelled running up to him. "Is your son safe?"

"Yes, he's with his mother." Richard clamped his hand on Mattias' shoulder. "Report."

"Well the fight is over. It stopped when Vincent went running into the forest. The young-ones didn't know what to do without his presence. We have about forty dead. Most of them were crushed by the castle wall collapsing. The rest are just injured, but nothing life threatening."

"You don't have a scratch on you," Richard said looking his general over.

"Stayed in the trees under cover with my cross bow. I flashed out of the way when something came near," he shrugged. "You know, the usual."

"I forgot that was your usual strategy."

"Well someone has to cover your arses."

"Get Martouf and Lantash and any other available elf and start a clean-up. I'm going after my brother."

"Where the hell was Lampros when all this was going on? I didn't see him."

"Chained up."

"Did your sister get kinky?"

"I really don't need to hear crap like that. Speaking of, tell Martouf to release him when you find him, if Trixie hasn't already done it."

"Will do boss," Mattias said smiling at Richard. He gave Richard a salute before taking off to find his fellow generals.

Shaking his head, Richard looked towards the forest. He could still sense his brother in the Elven realm and it wouldn't be long before he found him. Smiling at that thought Richard started heading towards the forest. What he was going to do with his brother once he caught up to him, he had no idea.

Chapter Forty-Five

Richard slowly walked into the dark forest. Keeping his wits about him, he used all his senses to detect his brother. Vincent was still in the forest. Richard could sense that much. However, glancing around he couldn't see him. Closing his eyes Richard concentrated on his brother tuning out all other noises. Taking a step forward he heard the leaves crunch under his boot, which would give his position away. Opening his eyes, he looked to the ground, tracking had never been his strong suit that was Mattias' department. He could see crunched leaves everywhere, since the forest had seen a lot of action today. Trying to track Vincent that way would be an impossible task.

Putting his shields up he slowly walked further into the forest scanning the area around him and listening to anything that would indicate his brother was near. The problem Richard faced was his brother was unpredictable with his power steeling. God only knew what powers he currently possessed and it made Richard feel uneasy, even with his shields up. He wasn't scared of his brother, not by a long shot, but he also didn't want to end up dead because he was taken unaware either.

He stepped on something that didn't feel like leaves and looked down to see the cursed necklace his brother was so fond of. Had Vincent dropped it, or was this a trap? Releasing his shield, he crouched down to retrieve the item. When he picked it up he froze hearing a blast hit the tree behind him sending splinters of bark showering all over him. Raising his head, he saw his brother standing about ten meters away next to a tall tree with a lightning bolt in his hand. So, it had been a trap and his brother was poised to strike again.

"Bollocks to it," Richard muttered as he slowly stood up, placing the necklace in his pocket. He armed himself with his own bolts of light. If he was going to die, then he was going to. His son would be the new king and was currently well protected. He had nothing to worry about in that area, he just had to concentrate on the here and now. He knew that power wise he had nothing to worry about, being the king he would always be more powerful than the other elves. No matter how powerful a being was, a fight with him would always be risky. His brother could still take him out if he wasn't careful and he didn't want to cheat and freeze his brother. Not yet any way.

Richard slowly started walking towards his brother, watching the elf's every move. He knew it wouldn't be long before he was dodging bolts. He was waiting for his brother to make the first move, even though all his anger was telling him to just take the bastard out. He spotted his brother releasing a bolt of light and moved the top half of his body slightly left watching the bolt as it flew right past his head smashing into a tree. Richard could feel the heat of it as it whizzed past his head.

"Is that the best you got," he taunted his brother. He threw a bolt of his own, which Vincent had to duck to miss.

"No," Vincent replied throwing another bolt which was intercepted by Richard with a bright blast of light.

Slightly blinded by the light Richard was caught unaware as a blast impacted his shoulder, where the bullet wound was. The agony of it brought him to his knees and made him catch his breath. Releasing a small breath, he lifted his eyes to see his brother slowly walking towards him with a look of triumph on his face. He couldn't believe the gall of his brother, thinking he had the upper hand. Richard waited until his brother was a foot away from him, even though he noticed a bolt of light sitting on the palm of his brother's hand.

"So the powerful Richard has fallen, now to finish you and take your place." Vincent raised his hands to release the bolts at him. He suddenly stopped in his tracks gasping for breath. He felt like he was choking. Richard must be using his power on him.

Richard slowly stood, not once releasing the choke hold he had on his brother. He eased it slightly so his brother could at least breathe a little. Taking a step forward Richard now stood over his brother. The power flowing from him brought Vincent unwillingly to his knees.

"You were saying little brother."

"Richard just listen to me for one second," Vincent said through gritted teeth.

"And why the hell should I do that?"

"Richard, you haven't been here in years."

"Nor would I be now, had you not put my sons' life in danger," Richard said with a snarl. "What do you have to say about your actions?" he snapped pushing more of his power over his brother.

"I AM YOUR KING," Vincent yelled trying to overpower his brother.

Richard laughed coldly "You are clearly not my king, so what are you king of exactly?"

He released his power and the hold he had over his brother. "You are pathetic," he snarled and turned slowly and started to walk off.

Taking the opportunity Vincent lunged for his brother. Hearing his approach, Richard turned and using his power grasped his brother by the throat, holding him in place. A move worthy of a Jedi, had it not been a sith trait. He smiled to himself, remembering his earlier conversation with his sister. He had seen Star Wars and quite liked the movies except he wouldn't tell her that. Narrowing his silver eyes at Vincent, Richard walked slowly around his brother, never taking his eyes off him.

"Will you never learn? You are prince of the autumn elves, clearly that has not changed. So tell me what exactly are you a king of, because it is not the Elves?" Richard stopped in front of his brother awaiting an answer that did not come, so Richard continued. "It would seem that in my absence you took it upon yourself to rule. However, you did not and do not have the power for the task because you are not the true king of elves, let alone anything else. As usual, you wanted what was not yours to have. You are still a pathetic, selfish, ignorant moron. You have always been."

"Moron?" Vincent said looking at his brother confused. He had never heard the word before.

"Never mind that," he snapped starting to lose his patience. Richard tightened the grip he still had on his brothers' throat. "You my dear brother, tried to kill my son. It would seem like you have forgotten just how evil, I myself can be. So tell me brother, why I shouldn't just kill you where you stand?"

Vincent looked at his brother, feeling his panic rising. He had been so consumed with gaining more power for himself at any cost, he'd forgotten what his brother had been like before he met Isabella. Never mind what Richard had done when Vincent had tried to seduce Isabella. Shuddering at the memory, he tried to think of something, anything that might buy him some time. Or at the very least, distract his brother enough for him to attempt to get away. "You are a good man." Vincent finally said.

Richard smirked at his brother "There is one problem with that statement, brother".

Vincent was confused with what his brother had said, but that quickly turned to fear as electrical light flashes started shooting from his brother's hands.

"I am not currently a man," said Richard smirking as he raised his hands. An eye for an eye as the old saying went.

Chapter Forty-Six

Isabella knelt beside her son whose gaze was still transfixed on his grandmother. Even when they lowered the chains, his gaze hadn't faltered.

"Jordan focus," she snapped, clicking her fingers in his face. His eyes focussed on her.

"Mummy," Jordan squeaked, immediately throwing his arms around her neck. He squeezed so tight she was surprised she could still breathe and hoped he didn't break anything.

"Ok sweetie let mummy go, she needs to breathe" she said reluctantly. It had been a long time since he had called her mummy and it always made her feel warm inside. She ran her palm down Jordan's head and face as he released her and placed a kiss on his forehead. Martouf, Lantash and Mattias joined them in the dungeon.

"That looks nasty," Martouf said as he looked down at Jordan's wrists. Crouching down he gently picked up the shackles and undid them before heading over to release Lampros from his.

"Can you stand?" Isabella asked her son as she started to get up.

"I don't know? Am I dreaming or dead or something?" Jordan asked totally confused.

"Why would you ask that?" Isabella said as she looked to where her son was pointing. "Yes that's Nan and no you're not dead or dreaming," she said smiling.

"Good. I didn't think I would be in this much pain in heaven or it would look like.... what happened to the wall?" Jordan asked as he noticed the big gaping hole.

"Would you believe me if I said your Dad decided to help your Uncle renovate?"

"Not really," Jordan replied, slowly getting to his feet. He was surprised he was even able to stand. He took a step towards his beloved grandmother, grabbing her in a tight embrace. God he had missed her.

"Ok now, that's enough of that," Christina said as she placed a kiss on his cheek. Placing an arm gently around his waist she continued, "Let's get you out of here and to the neutral realm hospital."

"Mum, I don't think he is strong enough to flash yet," Isabella said concerned for her sons' health and safety.

"Don't worry sweetheart, he is just tagging along." She had taken a few steps towards the doors when suddenly they heard an ear splitting scream. "What the hell was that."

"You mean who the hell is that," Isabella said as she ran towards the hole in the wall. She stood next to Martouf and looked at the direction the sound was coming from freezing in fear when her eyes hit the forest. She looked at Martouf but couldn't work out what was happening. "What is it?"

He looked at her and back to the forest. "Can anyone else feel that?" he asked looking at everyone in the room. All the elves nodded.

"What is going on?" Isabella's frantic tone had Martouf turning towards her. He frowned not understanding why she was worried, then he clicked.

"The king is currently gaining more powers."

"What!" Isabella said looking at Martouf. "Whose?"

"My guess would be Vincent's," Martouf replied shrugging.

"How?"

"Most likely the same way Vincent took Jordan's," Lampros chimed in. "However I don't think the realm will save Vincent, since it's the King doing the taking."

"You are kidding aren't you?" Isabella asked, looking at everyone in turn. The fact that her mother was shaking her head had her worried. Looking back to Martouf she continued, "So what will happen to Vincent?"

"He will most likely die. In the same way he has made others die."

"And what the hell will that do to my husband?" Isabella screeched placing her hands on her hips.

"I have no idea my queen," Martouf said with regret.

"Well can't any of you do something?"

"There is nothing we can do. We just have to let things happen."

"Like hell," Isabella said just before she flashed from the room.

"Martouf?"

"Yes, Princess," he said turning to face Christina.

"You did that on purpose."

"I only spoke the truth. There is nothing that *we* can do. However, your daughter is another matter." Martouf said as he smiled at Christina. "Come on let's get our prince some medical attention. I'm pretty sure his mother will have all our hides if we are still here when they return."

Chapter Forty-Seven

Isabella appeared in the middle of the dark forest and grabbed onto the nearest tree for balance. It had been a while since she had flashed anywhere. She had to cover her ears quickly as the sounds of Vincent's screams sent shivers through her. The thought of her son going though that pain filled her with anger. She headed over to where the sound was coming from. The flashing lights in the distance was a clue on where to find her husband.

It wasn't long before Isabella could see both her husband and brother-in-law. A horrible sight greeted her. Vincent was on the forest floor withering and screaming. Her husband stood over him and had a look of joy on his face. Isabella clutched her stomach wanting to be sick. She had never seen that look on Richard's face while doing something so horrible or cruel to someone. No matter what the reason. Even the poor trees were suffering with the scorch marks they now possessed. She was surprised they hadn't caught alight.

She had to stop this, but how? Edging a bit closer, she looked around for options. She could double back and get behind Richard but startling him might cause her to accidently get zapped. Flashing behind him could have the same effect and looking at Vincent she really didn't want that. Rubbing her hands on the bum of her jeans she paused. "I'll zap him myself," she whispered.

Richard was getting so drunk on the power he was taking from his brother he didn't even notice his screams. Never mind the bolt of light that almost knocked him on his arse. Pain shot through his body, as his shoulder had yet again been hit. He immediately noticed the second he stopped using his power to drain Vincent. The loss of that feeling would have usually worried Richard but he was geared up with a bolt of light to fire at whoever it was that had attacked him. Raising his hand in the direction the bolt had come from, he stopped dead.

"Isabella," he whispered, slightly shocked.

Vincent feeling relieved for the distraction, decided to take the opportunity to get the hell out of there. Casting one last look at his brother, he flashed.

"Damn it," Richard said. He hit the nearest tree when he caught site of his brother disappearing. He looked back at his wife. "Isabella, what the hell are you doing here?"

"Don't you dare take that tone with me," she yelled storming towards her husband. "Just because I stopped your little cat and mouse game."

"Isabella. He almost killed our son."

"And you almost killed him so tell me something," she said as she stopped in front of her husband.

"Anything," he said tracing a finger down her cheek.

"Are you a cold blooded murderer?"

"No, why would you ask that?" he said shocked.

"Because you were about to become one and I couldn't have that." She rested her head on the shoulder that wasn't injured. "Crap, I hit your bad shoulder," she said looking back up into his face.

Richard shrugged with his good shoulder "Well you know how it is, you see a weakness and use it to your advantage."

"It wasn't like that," she said playfully slapping his arm.

"Maybe not, but don't forget it," he chastised.

"So what are we going to do about Vincent?"

"Nothing for now. I can't sense him in the realm, so for now we will not worry about that. How is Jordan?"

"He will live. Mum should have taken him to the neutral realm hospital."

"Well I guess we had better head there then. I think I might need my shoulder looked at. Everyone keeps trying to take my arm off today," Richard said kissing the top of his wife's head. Isabella just smiled at him as she wrapped her arms around his waist.

Chapter Forty-Eight

Isabella giggled watching her husband hiss with pain as his shoulder was being bandaged up. The hospital room they were in was like any other hospital room, clean and sterile. No machines were beeping away however, which was a good thing. Sitting on the bed next to her son she observed his facial features. He looked shocked and confused, like a lost little boy.

"Are you alright, sweetheart?"

"No" Jordan said flatly looking at his mother. "I ache all over, my wrists are out of action for a few weeks, I have been basically tortured by a psycho and I can't believe my grandmother is actually alive and kicking. Never mind the fact that I am also stuck in this bloody place."

"It won't be that bad, I had to do it when I was your age?"

"Really?" he said giving his mother a strange look.

"Yes really, why are you looking at me like that?"

"Why do you look younger?"

"Technically I am, the joys of the call of the rose being set off, it resets your age back to twenty-five."

"Aint that going to cause some problems back home?"

"Yes I guess it will," Isabella replied biting her lip.

"I have something for that," a male voice said from the doorway.

"Daddy," Isabella said jumping off the bed and hugging her father. "Where the hell have you been, we could have used your help."

"To do what? Magically heal Jordan's wrists."

"Well to start with," Isabella muttered.

Tristan kissed his daughters head and made his way over to his shocked looking grandson.

"Hey champ, I take it they didn't tell you I was still alive either by the look on your face."

"No," Jordan said giving his grandfather a hug. He really didn't know how much more he could take before he snapped and ended up in a looney bin.

"Here," Tristan said handing a piece of parchment to his daughter.

"What's this?" she said, taking the item from her father.

"A glamour spell."

"Aww shit yeah," Isabella had forgotten her Dad had this. Not only did she know how to cast it, but also knew that everything she would need would be at Rose Manor.

"As much as I love family reunions we really should be heading to the Elven castle to get Jordan settled in, before Isabella heads back to the human realm," Richard said as he stood. His shoulder had finally finished being seen to.

"You're not going with Mum?"

"No, I will be staying here a couple of weeks. We need to get you settled and start the training that I should have done before you got here. Plus, there is the Autumn Elves castle to rebuild so come on, chop, chop people, let's get a move on." Richard clapped and winced in pain. "Stuff it," he said as he left the room. Everyone else followed after him.

Chapter Forty-Nine

Isabella stood in the bedroom of the neutral realm that linked to Jordan's bedroom in the human realm. She flashed there with her son and husband, her parents were not too far behind. She hadn't realised that saying goodbye was going to be so hard. She didn't want to leave her son but she had to get back to the girls and see how Charlotte was doing. She decided against telling Jordan about what had happened to Charlotte, knowing he would worry himself sick. There was nothing he could do any way, never mind the fact that he couldn't pass through to the human realm until the five years was up. God only knew what they were going to tell the girls about Jordan's absence.

Walking up to her son, she grabbed him and hugged him so tight she was surprised he could still breathe.

"I love you," she whispered.

"I love you too Mum and besides from what I understand, you can come and go as you please, it's me who is stuck here."

"True," she said grabbing his head so she could kiss his cheek.

"So what are you going to tell my lovely sisters about my sudden disappearance?"

"I have no idea. I will just have to think of something when the time comes. I shan't worry about it for now. You just stay safe."

"I will," Jordan smiled and kissed his mother's forehead.

Isabella looked at her husband with a sly look on her face.

"Oh dear," Christina said looking at her daughters' face. She had seen that look before.

"What is it?" Jordan asked in confusion.

"You my darling, might just end up with some more siblings."

"I so didn't need to hear that. God Nan, getting visuals now. Yuck," Christina just laughed at her grandson.

"Mother stop it," Isabella said giving her mother a friendly slap on the arm, before giving her a big hug. "Love you mum," she said kissing her cheek.

Turning to Richard she wrapped him in a fiercely tight hug and gave him a quick kiss so she didn't embarrass their son. "I will see you in a couple a day's," and with that she was gone.

Vincent stood at the edge of the Elven mortal realm portal. With all that had happened he had to lie low for a while.

Flashing from his brother had taken a lot of his power. He had gone to a set of witches to get a potion made that wouldn't allow his brother to sense exactly where he was in the human realm. He could be right next door, but his brother would think he was across the ocean in Australia or America. Power had been their payment for the potion. The fact that Richard had taken some of his powers also didn't help. Flashing back to the castle to collect Sonya had also drained him, but he couldn't leave her behind. As much as his mind had said leave her and go, his body had argued. He found himself back at his boudoir, which was still intact.

So here he was once again standing by the portal to the human realm. He knew he would be back, just as soon as he had a plan. His brother was still pissed at him and Vincent truly believed that he would have killed him, had he not flashed when Isabella turned up. Not even Vincent had seen his brother that angry and he had to admit, it scared the shit out of him. Even more so since his brother's movements had still been under his control.

His plans had not changed, he still desired to be King of the Elven realm. He just had to plan things a little better. After all he still had three nieces' he could use, but that would have to wait.

"Let's go," he said grabbing Sonya's hand and stepping through the portal.

Dear Reader,

Thank you for taking the time to read my book. I hope you have enjoyed reading it as much as I have enjoyed writing it. Please feel free to leave a review about the book, even if it's just a few words to say what you thought or who your favourite character was.

As many times as this book has been proof read, there is bound to be a couple of mistakes that have managed to squeeze through. If you do happen to notice anything, please let me know by email at: chanellenash23@gmail.com

If you liked this book and would like to hear about future books in the series, you can follow me on Twitter or Facebook.

https://Twitter.com/chanellenash

www.facebook.com/authorchanellenash

Acknowledgements

A big thank you to all my family and friends who encouraged me throughout the writing of this book.

A special thank you to Kylie who has been there offering advice and encouragement whenever I hit little pitfalls while writing this book.

An extra big thank you to Nick, for without him the character of Lampros wouldn't have had such an unusual name.

About The Author

Photo curtesy of Tanya K Photography

As a child Chanelle loved to make up bedtime stories for her youngest siblings, telling them to pick characters and then would work them all into a story.

Born in London, Chanelle moved to Australia when she was thirteen with her parents and four younger siblings. But still continues to go between countries.

Currently residing in Perth, Western Australia. She shares a house with her youngest sibling and their Dog Demetrius and Cat's Smoke, Jensen & Shadow.

When not working at her part time job, she can be found spending time with family and friends, writing stories or letters, reading, doing genealogy and listening to music.

www.ingramcontent.com/pod-product-compliance
Lightning Source LLC
Chambersburg PA
CBHW071622030726
47598CB00001B/390